My Uncle Dudley

NOVELS BY WRIGHT MORRIS IN BISON BOOK EDITIONS
Date of first publication at the left

WRIGHT MORRIS

My Uncle
Dudley

University of Nebraska Press
Lincoln

Copyright 1942 by Wright Morris
Printed in the United States of America

Library of Congress Cataloging in Publication Data
Morris, Wright, 1910–
  My uncle Dudley

  "Bison book."
  Reprint of the ed. published by Harcourt, Brace, New York.
  I. Title.
[PZ3.M8346My9] [PS3525.07475]   813'.5'2   75–5696
ISBN 0–8032–5804–6

First Bison Book printing: 1975

Bison Book edition published by arrangement with the author. Origi-
nally published in 1942 by Harcourt Brace Jovanovich, Inc., New York.

For
BIRD

This is the grass that grows
wherever the land is and the water is

Contents

The Roundup

I

WHEN it was cold we walked around. When it was morning the pigeons came and looked but when nothing happened walked away. When it was warm we sat in the sun. Cars came down Sunset and when the light was red we could see the good-looking women inside. When it was hot the pigeons left the square. They made a great noise and spilled shadows everywhere, on my Uncle Dudley looking up at them. He looked off where they would come back just as they did. He waited till the last one came down, then he looked at me.

"You had enough milk and honey?" he said.

"I guess I've had enough," I said.

We got up and walked across the street. A boy selling papers held one out and my Uncle Dudley stopped to read. A fellow named Young had just won twenty-five thousand bucks. He'd swum all the way from Wrigley's island to a place right on the coast. There was a picture of him still covered with lard.

"You chew gum?" said Uncle Dudley.

"Sure," the boy said.

"Look what you've done," said Uncle Dudley, "look what you've done—ain't you ashamed?" We all looked at the fellow still covered with lard. Yesterday, it said, he hadn't a cent. Now he had twenty-five thousand bucks.

"Paper?" said the boy.

"No," Uncle Dudley said. We walked through the pigeons and crossed the square. We walked up Main street past the City Hall. The hock shops were just putting out their signs—Buck Jones was at the Hippodrome. Uncle Dudley looked in a mirror on a door. When he was in shape he was like an avocado, when he wasn't he was like a pear. Now he was mostly like a pear. We walked on down to a corner in the sun. "If I could lay my own eggs—" said my Uncle Dudley very loud, "if I could lay my own eggs I'd like it here!"

"Ain't it the goddam truth," said a man. My Uncle Dudley looked at him. The man looked back and Uncle Dudley smiled and felt where he kept his cigars. Then the light changed and the man walked away.

We crossed to be on the shady side. A fellow with tattooed arms was making hot cakes in a window, a row of bacon sizzled on the side. On one arm he had a man and on the other arm a woman—where the woman was his arm was shaved. Except her head and other places women have hair. She was a red-headed woman and had two diamond rings.

4

A man chewing a toothpick stopped to look at her too. He took the toothpick out and pressed his face to the glass. Bubbles were showing in the dough and the smell of bacon came out in the street—the fellow turned the cakes and they were the tough kind. He stacked them on a plate and set them aside. He poured three more on the griddle and wiped his hands. Then he picked up the plate and walked to the end of the counter, unrolling his sleeves before he sat down. He buttoned the one on the red-headed woman and began to eat.

"If I could lay my own eggs—" said Uncle Dudley, and he looked at the man as if he could. But the one with the toothpick didn't seem to hear. He kept looking inside at the new cakes on the griddle. The fellow at the counter began to eat very fast.

We crossed back to the sunny side. Near the corner there was a crowd looking at a doughnut machine; a woman was working it and wearing rubber gloves. The doughnuts went by on little trays and she sugared them. When she got ahead of the machine she held up two cards—one said 2 for 5, the other one said GOOD FOR YOU. "A wonderful thing!" my Uncle Dudley said. The door was open and the woman looked at him. She put down the cards and leaned on the doughnut machine. "If I was a machine," went on Uncle Dudley, "if I was a doughnut or nickel machine—" He looked around and everybody looked at him. The man with the toothpick came in close

5

and chewed on it. "If I could just lay my own—doughnuts," Uncle Dudley said.

"Ain't it the goddam truth," said the same man.

"Harry—" said Uncle Dudley, cuffing the man on the arm, "come have one on the Kid and me—a little farewell. We're leavin this wonderful land—this sunshine. We're goin home."

"Bygod," said the man, "I sure wish I was too." He was a tall man and used to wearing overalls. His thumbs kept feeling for the straps, scratching his chin.

"And now that we're leavin," said Uncle Dudley, "we never felt better in our life. We never felt better —did we, Kid?"

"Never!" I said.

"Mister—" said the man with the toothpick, "you sound like a Eastern man?"

"Right!" said Uncle Dudley. "Chicago's our home. . . ."

"Good old Chi?"

"Good old Chi!"

"I'm a Chicago man too," he said.

"My friend," said Uncle Dudley, "—that I knew."

"Not right in Chicago—more like Oak Park. Used to drive in Sundays to Lincoln Park—"

"Lincoln Park! Spring in Lincoln Park. No green in the world like Lincoln Park—boats on the lagoon—"

"Not on the lagoon—"

6

"Harry," said Uncle Dudley, "permit me—in my time—"

"Lived in Oak Park ten years—"

"Boats—" said Uncle Dudley, "on the old lagoon. No green in the world like the green in that park. And that's the green on the back of a bill. What I seen out here all that green's back there too."

"When you leavin, Mister?"

"Tomorrow," Uncle Dudley said. "Kid and I just now on our way to the *Times*. Put in a little ad—driving back, have big car. Too big for us, glad to share it with few friends. Share gas an oil—help us all some that way. Must be plenty men here like to get back to old Chi. Only trouble is Kid and I won't have room. How much room, Kid?" he said. "How much room we got?"

"Well—" I said.

"Not much—maybe two—three. Want it to be nice—southern route all the way. Be in New Orleans in time for Mardi Graw. Any you men been to the Mardi Graw?"

"Thought about goin," said the Oak Park man, "—one fall."

"The Mardi Graw," said Uncle Dudley, "is not in the fall."

"How much?" said a man.

"The Mardi Graw?"

"Good old Chi—"

"That—" said Uncle Dudley, "Kid and I'd like

7

your opinion on. Kid and I think twenty-five—
twenty-five do the trick. Not tryin to make any
money. Just gas—gas an oil."

"What kinda car?"

"Big car—but easy on gas. Very easy on gas. What
we been gettin, Kid—?"

"Eighteen and twenty," I said.

"Time I come out," said a man, "didn't get any
more than ten. Goddam car was like a long leak on
the road. We was 'fraid to get outa town . . ."

"Ring job—need the carbon out. When was it, Kid,
we had the carbon out?"

"Last week," I said.

"Well—" said Uncle Dudley, "got to get on with
that ad. Want to get out of town by noon. Since you
men think twenty-five O.K.—twenty-five goes in the
ad. First come first served. Too bad can't—"

"Twen-fife dolls?"

"To Chicago—all the way."

"Dee-troit?"

"Right next door. Fine town—right next door."

"Twen-fife dolls?" Uncle Dudley looked at him.
He was a big man in a brand new suit. He stood very
straight like it fit pretty tight.

"Detroit," said Uncle Dudley, "—maybe five dollars more."

"More?"

"More."

The big man looked at him. Then his mouth was

8

open and his eyes half closed—he finished counting and looked out again. "Twen-fife dolls?"

"Chicago—" Uncle Dudley said. The big man smiled and reached down in his pants. It pulled the buttons open and he had to stop and button up, then reach down in his pants again. He had a small roll of brand new tens. He counted off three into Uncle Dudley's hand.

"Right negs door?" he said. Uncle Dudley nodded and smoothed the bills. They were so new they all made a frying sound.

"You can never tell," said my Uncle Dudley, "—bygod you can never tell." He was just talking to himself like no one was around. "Old as I am," he said, "I still can't tell." The big man took off his hat and grinned. Something made him blush and the color showed through his hair, it went clear back where his head started down again. "Glad to meet you, Harry," Uncle Dudley said. "My name's Osborn—Dudley Osborn."

"Hansen—" said Mr. Hansen, and put on his hat.

"You're a lucky man," said Uncle Dudley, "—a very lucky man." And he shook Mr. Hansen's hand and slapped his arm. Mr. Hansen was wearing a pin and it fell off. It said, Visit Minnesota—Land O' Lakes. Mr. Hansen had more in his pocket and he gave me one, Uncle Dudley one. The man from Oak Park wanted one but Mr. Hansen just looked back. Uncle Dudley took out his fountain pen and one of his

9

T. Dudley Osborn cards and we all moved back so he could write on the glass. He put the card right where the woman was looking out. Under Dudley Osborn he wrote Biltmore Hotel, and on the back Mr. Hansen's receipt. "And now," said Uncle Dudley, "—twenty-five from thirty, right?"

"—negs door," Mr. Hansen said.

"Hmmm—" said Uncle Dudley, and walked in by the doughnut machine. He bought a half dozen doughnuts just plain and then three with the powdered sugar; the woman got red and put on more sugar than she should. Then he bought two White Owls and came outside with the change. Mr. Hansen took off his hat and put it on again. "Well—" said Uncle Dudley, handing him five, "come by early—want to get away early." Mr. Hansen gave me another button and patted my head. "Well—" said Uncle Dudley. Mr. Hansen grinned and walked away. Uncle Dudley didn't wait to see where but turned, and we walked away too. We stopped once and looked at shoes, once we looked at boy's hats. We stopped once where a movie was showing and looked at the signs. We crossed the street and then we stopped and looked back. Uncle Dudley stood on the curb and rocked at the knees. When he saw one that was really all right he rocked at the knees. I looked up and down for her and then I saw her on the corner; she was looking back our way but not at me.

"Should we buy a car now—or should we eat?" said Uncle Dudley.

"Let's eat first," I said.

"O.K.," he said. "Let's eat."

We went in where a man was frying eggs. His back was turned and his neck very white where it came out of his yellow underwear. He went on talking to someone sitting behind. "Hell, Natchez—" he said, "if you can't who the hell could?" The man sitting behind didn't say. "Slide around here," said the cook, "so I don't have to talk so loud," and then he put the man's plate of eggs beside me. The man behind the stove coughed, then he stood up. He was tall and had a coat with a real fur collar and his hair was long and curly at the ends. He came over and sat on the stool beside me. His nails were clean and he sat with his hands like he was going to pray.

"Natchez," said the cook, "you like a side a ham —more coffee?" he said.

"It's getting so, Roy," Natchez said, "a good crook can't make an honest living—two cent poker, half a day to make a dime." He looked at Uncle Dudley.

"Pair of ham and eggs," Uncle Dudley said. Natchez drank his coffee black, leaving in the spoon. Roy took four eggs from a pan and cracked them on the edge of the griddle—he cracked two at the same time and in each hand. He spilled them clean on the griddle with just one hand.

"Man like you," said Uncle Dudley, "—chewin your own ashes around here. If you don't make money you gotta go where it is." Natchez put down his coffee and looked at him.

"What kind of man am I?" he said.

"You're tryin to be a slick basterd," Uncle Dudley said. "But you're only wearin off your finish slidin around here."

"Bygod—" said Roy, "now that's good. Bygod that's good as hell. Guess the old man sure picked you clean—huh, Natchez?" Natchez just shrugged—twisted his ring around and around. He tapped his nails and they made a hollow sound. "How you men like your eggs?"

"Up," I said.

"Nice an sunny," he said. "Real California eggs," he went on, "nice an sunny side up." Uncle Dudley took out a cigar and looked at him.

"If I could lay my own—" he began, then he stopped and looked at Natchez. "Be in New Orleans soon—just in time for the Mardi Graw." Roy slid the plates down the table and they stopped by me. I took the one with the most potatoes, smallest eggs. The ham was so thin it wouldn't lay flat without the potatoes. I left them there and began to eat the eggs.

"New Orleans?" said Natchez.

"On our way to Chicago. Nice town, New Orleans —warm, plenty of dough."

"Driving?"

"Only way we'd ever go. Only way to get the country—feel it," Uncle Dudley said. He put down his fork and squeezed a handful of air. "Western air—" said Uncle Dudley. Natchez finished off his eggs. Roy poured us all more coffee, slid down the glass of spoons. Natchez took it black but he put in too much sugar.

"Bygod—" said Roy, "sure wish I had some extra dough. Heard so dam much about New Orleans— what's it they call it, Mardi—?"

"Graw." Uncle Dudley looked up at him, then looked back at the door. A red-headed sailor with a small bag was standing there. He stood with his behind off to one side and kept his mouth shut chewing gum.

"How's them ham and eggs?" said Roy, very loud. "How's them home cooked ham and eggs?"

"Best I've ever had," said Uncle Dudley. "Eggs fried in country butter is really good." Roy stared at him and Uncle Dudley smacked his lips. He took a piece of bread and wiped the grease off his plate.

"Yeah—" said Roy, and the sailor came in and sat down. The red hair on his chest grew right up to his neck where it stopped like grass along a sidewalk would.

"New Orleans—" Uncle Dudley was saying, "there's one town a man should never miss. Kid and I go out of our way just to be drivin through—"

"Just you an the Kid?" said Natchez.

"Most the time—except on a long haul. On a long haul Kid an I like some company around. Got a big, roomy car—helps while away the time. Everybody buys a little gas, helps everybody along."

"Gas?" said Roy.

"Little gas an oil—everybody sharin expenses all the way. Kid an I furnish the car an you help furnish the gas an oil."

"Bygod—" said Roy, "now that sounds O.K. Bygod if I had some coin I'd jump at that—"

"Just on our way now to put in a little ad. Pick up a couple boys who'd really like to go east. Must be plenty in this hole like to get back in the east."

"Omaha—?" said Roy.

"Sure—all points east. Kid an I live in Chicago—Omaha right next door."

"Bygod—sure like Omaha. Was a kid in Omaha. Keep tellin my wife, 'Hell, Mabel, what good this goddam sun do me? My face paler'n my behind. When I was a kid in Omaha I was . . .'"

"Bowl of oatmeal," the sailor said.

"How much gas—" said Roy, scooping oatmeal, "—you figure to Omaha?" Uncle Dudley took out his pen. Then he took out one of his cards and wrote Biltmore under his name.

" 'bout twenty is what I figure to New Orleans—same to Omaha."

Natchez was picking his teeth. He had a little gold toothpick in a silver case and it slipped inside like a

14

sword. When he faced the light he had a thin black moustache but side on you couldn't see a thing. "What car you drivin?" he said. "Twenty bucks buys a lot of gas."

"Ever buy gas—" said Uncle Dudley, "in Wagon Wheel, Socorro? Ever buy gas in Caballo, Malaga, Corona, Alamogordo?" Natchez shook his head. We hadn't either as yet but probably would in time. Uncle Dudley looked across at the sailor and the sailor looked him back.

"Sounds O.K. to me," the sailor said. Uncle Dudley looked at Natchez.

"Bygod—" said Roy, "if it wasn't for Mabel—"

"When you leavin?" said Natchez.

"Morning—" said Uncle Dudley, "try to get away early, want to be on our way by noon." The sailor stopped eating his oatmeal and looked right straight ahead. He was adding up something and blinked his eyes when he got at the end.

"Warm, southern route all the way," said Uncle Dudley. "Back home just in time for spring. Nothin like Lincoln Park in the spring. Remember Lincoln Park in the spring, Kid?"

"Boy!" I said. I stopped eating and looked around. I looked out at the street like the park was there and the pigeons walking around. The sailor made a noise with his spoon. He had blue eyes and was the kind Uncle Dudley called a clean-lookin kid.

"You drivin east?" he said.

"Points east," said Uncle Dudley.

"You got any room?"

"Well—" said Uncle Dudley, "depends on the Kid —Kid likes room. Like room in a long haul. How about it, Kid—we got room?"

"Well—" I said.

"Where you goin?" said Uncle Dudley.

"Pittsburgh—"

"Hmmmm—right next door."

"That is if you're goin that far—if you're not, goin as far as you go."

"We're goin to Chicago—twenty-five to Chicago. Pittsburgh right—"

"Straight ahead," said Natchez.

"Sure," said Uncle Dudley, "right—on."

Natchez dropped a quarter on the counter. He put away his gold toothpick and looked a long time at his nails. Then he said, "Say we split the difference —say, seventeen-fifty?" Uncle Dudley squinted at his card. He turned it over and wrote on the back *Received from*—then, *for sharing expenses to Chicago.*

"Really prefer somebody goin all the way," he said. "like to have you along—but like a man to go all the way."

"Count me in," said the sailor. "You want the dough now?"

"Pardon me—" said Natchez, "but this gentleman and I—"

16

"My dough's on the counter," said the sailor, and unbuttoned his pants. He had a money belt on and had to half take off his pants.

"Well—" said Natchez. "Since money talks—"

"Now, now, boys," said Uncle Dudley. "Now—Now—" he said, and reached and took the two fives from Natchez. "Got to keep peace in the family—got to share and share alike. Can we find room for 'em, Kid?"

"Well—" I said.

"Sure—that's fine. Like a nice car full myself. An now, Mr.—"

"Ahearn," said the sailor, and handed some more new tens to Roy. Roy wiped his hands before he took them, then passed them along. Mr. Ahearn put his belt back on and buttoned up his pants.

"Received—" said Uncle Dudley, and wiggled the pen around, then he wrapped the card in one of Natchez fives and Roy passed it along. "And now—" said Uncle Dudley.

"Blake," said Natchez.

"Received—ten on account—from Mr. Blake," and he gave him a card.

"Biltmore?" said Natchez.

"Nice place—" Uncle Dudley said, "nice roomy lobby—make yourself at home."

"Where's it at?" said Mr. Ahearn.

"Funny thing—" said Uncle Dudley. "Yes *sir*, a really funny thing, but Kid an I been there a week an I still don't know where it is. Kid leads me around by the hand. If it wasn't for the Kid I'd never get there—where's it at, Kid?"

"Not far—" I said.

"Biltmore?" said Roy. "Hell, that's right up the street."

"Sure—"

"Sure," I said.

Natchez walked and stood in the door. His coat had wide padded shoulders and the bottom nearly reached the floor. He wore gray button spats and one of them was nearly new.

"Leavin in the morning?" he said, without turning.

"Want to be on the road by noon."

"I gotta lot to do," said Mr. Ahearn, and dropped a dime and walked out. Natchez watched him walk off down the street.

"Where the sailors get them nice behinds?" he said.

"It's a gift," Roy said. Natchez shrugged and looked at his hands. He took out his gold toothpick and cleaned one nail, then he put it away. He walked out and stood on the curb.

"Bygod if it wasn't for Mabel—" said Roy, and walked behind the stove. He began to wash dishes back there.

"What if there hadn't been one?" I said.

"There's always a Biltmore," said Uncle Dudley.

"A swell dump," said Roy, "Mabel likes to meet me

there and stand around." He came out and stood wiping his hands. He poured us more coffee and I sat and ate doughnuts while Uncle Dudley telephoned.

We stood on the corner of Sixth and Spring sizing the women up. They were pretty good right around here. When Uncle Dudley saw something he really liked he first always looked away. I used to wonder about that. Then I saw that made the women look at him and when he looked back there they were. And they all looked better that way. From right then on they even walked better and stopped so they stood the right way. They both sort of enjoyed it somehow. He liked them big and built high off the ground but sometimes he'd look at anything. Sometimes I thought they would too. But he had a good leg and with his hat off it was only the part in between. Which was more than I could say for some of them. Though I wasn't sure how I liked them yet. But Uncle Dudley said all of that would come in time. Like my knowing it wasn't how much a woman weighed—but where.

A man walked by with a sign on his back that said TRAVEL BY BUS AND SAVE. Uncle Dudley and I walked behind. In the middle of the block the man turned in but left his sign parked out in front. Another sign was nailed on the door. An old man with one leg leaned on his crutches and read all of the prices out loud. He wore a black derby and a black overcoat, and had black shoes with elastic sides. "Well, well—" said Uncle Dudley. "Guess we drive back after all— I thought you told me that the bus fare was cheap?"

"I guess I was wrong," I said.

"Hell—" said Uncle Dudley, "I'd take a man for twenty-five. Yes *sir*—clear to Chicago, all the way." The old man on crutches turned and looked at him. His face was like tanned leather and something smelled. "Yes *sir*, clear to Chicago—" Uncle Dudley said.

"How much for two?" said the man.

"A gentleman?"

"A gentleman."

"For two—" said Uncle Dudley, "Kid and I might make it forty-five."

"He's no bigger than the Kid," said the man, "and hell—I'm only half here!"

"Thought of that—" said Uncle Dudley.

"We're actors—we're in the Miracle Play."

"It didn't work?"

"How can I work?"

"Maybe forty-two fifty," Uncle Dudley said.

"But—" said the man. Uncle Dudley looked at me.

"Maybe you're right, Kid—" he said. "There just ain't room—no room for two."

"You just said—" said the man.

"Yes?"

"Forty-two fifty."

"Can you manage, Kid? They're willing to be crowded a little—but are you? I leave it to you."

"Well—" I said. Uncle Dudley took out a card. Under his name he wrote Biltmore, and under Biltmore Room 331.

"Mister—?"

"Demetrios," said the man.

"All now—" said Uncle Dudley, "or thirty now—the rest in the morning?" Mr. Demetrios made a sound with his teeth. His uppers hung down so I could see the rubber gums and he let them hang there, his tongue making the noise. "Well—" said Uncle Dudley. Mr. Demetrios leaned on his crutch. From under his arm he pulled a bag that snapped back on a rubber string. He pulled it out again and pried open the drawstring top. It was full of pennies and two rolls of bills. He counted off ten and then he stopped and took a very long look at me. I took a very long look at him. He counted off twenty more and Uncle Dudley gave it to me. "And now your friend's name?" said Uncle Dudley. Mr. Demetrios made the noise again.

"Pop—" he said.

"Pop?"

"Just Pop—we call him Pop." Uncle Dudley wrote down Pop. "He's no bigger than the Kid."

"Kid ain't so small."

Turning away, Mr. Demetrios spit.

"Biltmore—" said Uncle Dudley. "Make yourself at home."

"In the morning?"

"In the morning," Uncle Dudley said. Mr. Demetrios read the card over to himself out loud. The man running the bus station came outside and looked at us.

"What's goin on here?" he said.

"You gotta match?" said Uncle Dudley. He gave Uncle Dudley a match and watched him light his cigar. Uncle Dudley blew the smoke out slow and we walked away.

We had an orange drink at Fifth and Main. Uncle Dudley bought popcorn and we walked up toward the Biltmore, sat down on a bench in Pershing Square. We ate popcorn and looked at the hotel. It was a pretty smooth place with a man out in front with nothing to do but open doors. Pigeons came and ate from Uncle Dudley's hand. "How many we got?" he said.

"Five now," I said.

Uncle Dudley fed some popcorn to the squirrels. Some of the pigeons didn't have any tails at all, worn clean off like those on Halsted street. "How much that leave for a car?"

"About twenty dollars," I said.

"That enough?" said Uncle Dudley.

"That ain't enough," I said.

"Isn't—" said Uncle Dudley. I let it pass. "That's what you sold it for," went on Uncle Dudley.

"Buyin isn't sellin," I said.

"Well—I guess you're learnin," he said.

"That was a good car," I said. "Only two gallons of oil."

"Maybe he'll sell it back," Uncle Dudley said.

"It's not that good," I said. "No rubber on it—no lights—no brakes—no second gear."

"I could sit an hold it."

"Not all the way," I said. "An besides you can't hold everything." Uncle Dudley got up and walked away. He listened to a man giving a speech near the fountain and he clapped very loud when the man was through. Then he came back and looked at me.

"Sometimes—" he said, "I like it here."

"How much we got?" I said.

"We'll have about a hundred."

"That's just about gas," I said. Uncle Dudley walked away. He listened to another man talking about something and when he stopped said something to him. The man called Uncle Dudley one. By the time I got there the man was gone and Uncle Dudley was on the box. When he saw me he got down again.

"Well," he said.

"We got to get going," I said. We walked across the street and into the Biltmore while the man was holding the door. We crossed the lobby and went up the stairs. There was a long hall with lights shining on pictures and people sitting around. Uncle Dudley said the pictures stank. When he was young Uncle Dudley used to paint. He said he learned how to paint so he could paint right over the pictures his Dad had on the wall. We came back down to the lobby again. Uncle Dudley stopped at the desk and asked if he had any calls. "I'm driving east," he said, "driving east with a few friends." A man buying a cigar lit it and looked at him. "Good time to drive," said Uncle Dudley. "Cool on the desert—best time of year."

"Tch," said the man. "How I enfy you."

"Ha!" said Uncle Dudley. "Nothing fancy—just going home. Sharing expenses with a few friends—easier that way."

"Fery smart," said the man. "How I enfy you."

"You're going east?" said Uncle Dudley.

"New York—I titch in New York. I am a muzic titcher in New York," he said.

"My name's Osborn," said Uncle Dudley.

"I am Mr. Liszt," said Mr. Liszt. Uncle Dudley slowly shook his hand. Mr. Liszt was a good-looking man and beside him Uncle Dudley's pants weren't pressed. Mr. Liszt had glasses that made his eyes big and a ribbon hanging down to his coat.

"Now—" said Uncle Dudley. "If we weren't full—"

"Oh—too bat," said Mr. Liszt.

"Yes—you wouldn't be comfortable. Wouldn't mind myself but you professional men—"

"Ach—" said Mr. Liszt, "I ride anywhere. I haf rode across France in a car."

"France—" said Uncle Dudley.

"I ride in front. In New York I ride all ofer three in front."

"Well—" said Uncle Dudley.

"I be frank. I plan to titch here—no titching at all. I haf but fifty dollars between us and New York. I gif you haf an we ride three in front?"

"Chicago—" said Uncle Dudley.

"Chicago! I haf already titched in Chicago."

"Well," said Uncle Dudley. Mr. Liszt reached into his coat. He walked to the window and tipped his billfold to the light. Then he turned his back to Uncle Dudley and stood awhile. "Twenty-fife?" he said.

"Twenty-five," said Uncle Dudley.

Mr. Liszt came back with the bills in a small roll. "Count it," he said, "fife fifes." Uncle Dudley counted it. He felt in his pocket for a card but this one said JOE's DAIRY LUNCH. "Pleese—" said Mr. Liszt, "there is no neet. I count myself a fery goot chudge of men."

"That's very handy," said Uncle Dudley. Mr. Liszt smiled and wet his lips.

"Infaluble—" he said. Uncle Dudley put the bills away.

25

"Well—" said Uncle Dudley. "Biltmore—make yourself at home."

"Right here?"

"Oh—" said Uncle Dudley. "Yes—right here." Mr. Liszt smiled and put his hand on my back.

"Your poy?"

"My brother's kid."

"A fine lookink poy."

"He's a nice kid."

"Three of us—" said Mr. Liszt. "Riting in front—riting, riting, riting—"

"Well—" said Uncle Dudley, "Kid an I got to pick up the car."

"Ah!" said Mr. Liszt.

"Yeah—" said Uncle Dudley.

Mr. Liszt shook Uncle Dudley's hand very hard. In the lighter on the desk Uncle Dudley tried to light his cigar but it kept bouncing up and down like a rubber one. Uncle Dudley took it out and put it away. We stopped and looked at a potted plant near the door. A woman carrying a dog came in and we went out the revolving doors while they were still going and the smell of her was inside. We crossed the street and the pigeons followed us in the square. We walked around it once, then we stopped for an orange drink.

We had another orange drink on Fifth and Main. She was from North Platte and knew some people

Uncle Dudley knew there. She liked it here and then again she didn't, which was about the way I felt about it too. Uncle Dudley said he'd tell her folks she was looking fine. She gave us another drink free and we gave her the doughnuts we had. Uncle Dudley left her two-bits and we both walked off very fast.

We walked out Seventh street where we knew Agnes would be. She was still there in the lot on the corner, her front tires flat. Somebody had shined up her hood but nothing else. She still had her Michigan plates and no glass in the windshield, the cardboard I used against bugs said, MAKE OFFER—CHEAP. There was still no glass on the light where I'd cracked the steer. I crossed the street and stood alongside and nobody came out so I got in the seat, I put my hands on the steering wheel and my foot on the clutch. I made noises like little kids make and put her in high. She wouldn't stay there before but she stayed now. I felt the sawdust they'd put in her to make her shift. I could smell Uncle Dudley's cigar and feel his knee bumping mine and I knew that he couldn't hold her any longer and I'd have to shift. I could feel it down in my stomach when I did. I could feel my initial on the wheel and whether the clutch was dragging or not and if the timing gear would last until Santa Fe. I saw that they'd set her back so she read in five numbers now. I got out and let the door swing for she wouldn't close. I walked out in front and when I looked back she was still out of line—like a dog runs or a barge on the sewage canal. I crossed the street where Uncle Dudley was waiting for me.

"She was a good girl," he said, and we walked on by.

When we got to Alameda we turned right. On the sidewalk in front of a garage was a big car with little wire wheels, an old Marmon but she still had class. AIRPLANE ENGINE—SWEET RUNNER, the windshield said. We walked on by—there was even a tire on the spare. All of them held some air and the one up front had tread showing, retread maybe but showing anyhow. We crossed the street for a side view and she really was some wagon, belly right on the ground and a high, smooth-lookin hood. The little wire wheels did something to me somehow. We went back and walked by again and she had seven seats—could be eight with three riding in the front. I looked inside and the dash was keen as hell. She had a rear-end transmission and somehow I liked that too. We went on by and around the corner to a stand. Uncle Dudley had root beer and I had a bar.

"What's it worth, Kid," he said.

"Maybe ninety bucks," I said. "Maybe eighty—ninety bucks."

"What'll I offer?"

"Sixty," I said, "maybe go to seventy-five."

"Twenty-five down?"

"Twenty-five down," I said. Uncle Dudley bought

another White Owl and we went back. We stopped right in front and stood looking at it. The man looked at us and we didn't leave so he came out. He stood wiping his hands.

"Like a good wagon?" he said.

"Right now like a car," Uncle Dudley said.

"A three-thousand-dollar wagon—" said the man, not laughing. "Rubber up—perfect shape—fired to go."

"Blue book about seventy bucks," said Uncle Dudley.

"What?"

"Maybe less," Uncle Dudley said. "On a trade maybe eighty—cash deal fifty-five. I'm offerin fifty-five."

"Gee-*zus*-crist!" said the man.

"Make it fifty," said Uncle Dudley.

"The engine in there cost a thousand bucks to build—airplane engine—same goddam engine they used in the war. More goddam power than anything you ever seen. An you offer me—"

"Fifty bucks," said Uncle Dudley. The man wiped his hands. He threw the rag on the ground and started back into the garage. Then he turned—

"You really want that car—make me an offer—an honest offer?"

"How's she sound?" Uncle Dudley said. The man came back and got inside. He stepped on the starter and she turned right over, smooth. He raced her and she took it—no rap when she lagged.

"Pretty loose," I said.

"My god yes," said Uncle Dudley, "she'll bend both ways at the knees." The man let her idle a bit.

"Want to try it, Kid?" Uncle Dudley said.

"O.K.," I said. I got in and Uncle Dudley sat in the rear. The hood was so high I could hardly see over and when I stretched the pedals slipped away. But I horsed around until it felt all right. I tried the clutch and it felt clean. I let her out. The man gave me a hand at the corner to get her around. In high she picked up all right, no carbon ping.

"Better take it easy," said Uncle Dudley, "prob'ly get about six blocks to the gallon. If you poured it in with the engine runnin you'd never get it full."

"Listen that motor!" said the man.

"I can't help it," said Uncle Dudley. I couldn't either and she sounded all right. She had a nice throaty cough and when I gave it to her it was the nuts. When we went between sign boards she sounded like a racing car. I managed the next corner by myself, leaning on the wheel. On the next one it was easy and I had the knack. The brakes were wheezy but the pedal didn't get to the floor. When we stopped the man leaned forward and shut her off.

"Not much gas in her," he said.

"Not any more," said Uncle Dudley. "Well, Kid— is she still worth fifty bucks?"

"About," I said.

"Bygod!" said the man. "You can go to hell," and he got out.

"Not in this," said Uncle Dudley. "Cost too dam much," and he got out too. I didn't want to get out but Uncle Dudley coughed. "Well—" he said. "You're sure one dam fool if you think that freight car's money today. Who the hell wants a truck like that? Who the hell but me?"

"Listen," said the man, "seventy-five bucks cash."

Uncle Dudley shrugged and looked very sad. "I tell you what—I can use it—twenty-five down till I know it works."

"None of that," said the man, "cash—sixty bucks cash."

"If it's *cash*," said Uncle Dudley, "fifty stands." The man walked away. Uncle Dudley lit his cigar and we moseyed down the street. On the corner we stopped and Uncle Dudley lit his cigar again. Then we looked up and down the street, then back at the garage. The man was standing in the door waving at us. Uncle Dudley and me slowly moseyed back.

2

MY UNCLE DUDLEY stepped from the shower and drooled on the rug. He did five bending exercises, then stopped and felt for his heart—he had to feel around for it but it was there. He did five more and this time it showed. "I forget," he said. "Whether it should or whether it shouldn't." He did five more and wiped under his arms. In the glass he saw how really bad it was sideways—so he turned front on and flexed his arms. He had a good arm but it hung right off his neck. Uncle Harry used to say he had the longest neck he'd ever seen, Uncle Dudley being neck clear to the floor. It made his arms stick out like chicken wings. But he had a good calf so he wore knickers most of the time. He said there was just nothing like knickers for traveling in.

He took them from under the mattress and stood picking off lint. I got up and went to wet my hair. Uncle Dudley said girls would like my hair. I didn't know but since then I remembered to comb it and use some vaseline when it was around. That was funny since I didn't like girls anyhow. But Uncle

Dudley said to keep combing for there'd come a time.

Uncle Dudley took two face towels and one soap. We were up three floors but Uncle Dudley wanted to walk and look at the pictures on the stairs. On the first we stopped where we could see the lobby by peeking through some potted plants and ferns. Mr. Ahearn was standing near the door. He was in his sailor suit and standing like they did so you couldn't help notice their behinds. There was a small bag beside him on the floor. Right behind was Natchez and a tall thin man with three big bags between his legs. Natchez was tapping on his shoe with a cane. He wore a black muffler that covered up his front and made the curls stick out a little on his neck. Across the room Mr. Demetrios and a little man sat on a settee. The little man wore a bright green cap. Mr. Demetrios' crutches were across their laps and his leg was stretched out on three bags. The little man's legs didn't quite reach the floor. He sat very quiet with his hands in his lap watching Mr. Liszt walk up and down. At the door Mr. Liszt turned and looked quick at his bags.

Uncle Dudley took a towel out of his pocket and wiped his face. "Well—" he said.

"I'll go get the car," I said. Uncle Dudley took off his hat and wiped his head. I remembered when he used to look naked that way because his face below was so tanned. That was before he knew me. Now

33

he took it off when we sat in the park and the brown looked good with the white hair. Uncle Dudley wiped his face once more, then he folded the towel, put it away. We both walked out on the stairs. Mr. Liszt saw us first and he said "AAAHHH!" and then all of them saw us and stood up. I walked right through and nearly reached the door.

"I'll be goddam'd—" said Mr. Ahearn. "What is this car—a bus?" I just leaned on the door, looking out. I waited until Uncle Dudley began to laugh—then Mr. Ahearn. Then I went out.

She was right where I had left her on the grade. One tire was low but enough air to get around. I bought two eighty-cent luggage racks, a water bag, and five gallons of oil. Then I bought three tire shoes, a patch kit, and a pump. There was one tire iron and a jack under the seat. I put the luggage racks on each side and hung the water bag up front, then I got in and the battery was dead. But that was why I parked on the grade. So I let her roll and put her in gear, and she turned over without a cough. I went out Figueroa to a used tire place. I got three not so bad ones and two tubes for a buck and a half. I got some rope and tied two to the spare, the third one up front. Then I filled her up with cheap gas and came back.

But when I got in close the doorman wouldn't let

me park. I honked like hell and Uncle Dudley came out and sent the doorman to help with the bags. Everybody was laughing and looking pretty gay. Uncle Dudley was sparking around and Natchez was kidding Mr. Ahearn; every now and then he cuffed him on the seat. Only Mr. Hansen wasn't there. Instead of him was the tall thin man with the pile of bags. I got out and began to load them on. I got two on the bumper up front and two between the fender and the hood—the rest of the stuff fit in the racks on the side. All the time Uncle Dudley was busy carrying on. They flipped coins for seats and laughed and laughed when they thought they won, even Mr. Ahearn sitting on the spare thought he won too. Uncle Dudley could do that kind of thing. Mr. Liszt didn't know the game so they let him sit up front where he was, the tall thin man winning the place outside. "All aboard," Uncle Dudley was yelling and people stood on the curb to watch, making me wish Uncle Dudley wasn't as good as he was.

"*All* aboard?" I said, meaning Mr. Hansen.

"Go down Main street," Uncle Dudley said. I took it easy getting under way. I couldn't help think of Kansas City where the transmission fell out in the street, people still waving goodbye a block away. Uncle Dudley was singing *California—Here We Come* and everybody was gay like they were now— and then the transmission fell right out in the street.

The dam thing caught on the tracks and pushed the rear end right out of the car—holding up traffic and even stopping a train. We'd all just sat there till a policeman came along. "Slow along here," Uncle Dudley was saying, and I wondered why till I saw him wave. "Hey, Hansen!" he hollered. "Oh—Hansen." And there was Mr. Hansen standing in front of the doughnut machine. He had on his new suit and hat and a small trunk between his legs. I stopped and Uncle Dudley got out and brought up Mr. Hansen. "Gentlemen," said Uncle Dudley, "I leave it to you— are we going to leave Mr. Hansen behind?" Nobody said anything. "Just what I thought," said Uncle Dudley. "Give me your bag, Olie," he said. Mr. Hansen handed up his small trunk. By spreading Pop's legs Uncle Dudley got it in between the two spares— then he moved over and sat on it, Mr. Hansen taking the spare. But he was so big he had to sit facing the side and Mr. Demetrios' crutches crossed his lap. "All aboard?" said Uncle Dudley. Nobody said anything. "Fine!" he said. "O.K., Kid—let her roll." I let her roll, but very easy like. "Chicago—" yelled Uncle Dudley, "Chicago—here we come!"

"Dee-troit?" said Olie.

Uncle Dudley didn't say. He was down behind the seat lighting his cigar, then he looked up and blew the smoke on Olie's neck. Olie leaned out and looked at the pepper trees, the hills. Pasadena sloped up like a beach with bright little stones. "Right negs door," said Olie.

"Sure—" my Uncle Dudley said.

She felt good up through the floor board and through my shoe. She knocked a little on the rise— but that was cheap gas. I let her out a bit on the flat and at forty-five she was loose and idle, fifty-five drew her up where she was snug. When a car is snug she feels like a cat in your hands. And when you are snug with the car you purr right back.

Uncle Dudley was talking about Raton. Whenever we started off anywhere he thought of Raton. He didn't like Raton and he didn't like Albuquerque either. And from Albuquerque he went to Socorro— since it happened that way. He'd taken the wrong road out of Albuquerque and gone south. He was so glad to see Socorro he hadn't got over it yet, even though there was nothing there to see. Which was another reason he liked it pretty well. He liked Santa Fe better which had something to see, but it wasn't that part that he liked. He said it was the same about me. There was something to see but it wasn't that part that he liked.

Uncle Dudley was asking all of them where they were from. The thin man was Mr. Jeeves and he was from Peoria. Uncle Dudley didn't like Peoria at all. Anyone who's lived in South Bend, Cedar Rapids, or St. Joe would know why—providing they don't live there any more. "Where the hell you from?" said Mr. Jeeves.

"Everywhere," said Uncle Dudley. "I'm from a town before I get there—or I wouldn't go. Wouldn't run the risk of havin to stay on there."

"Thought you was from Chicago?" said Jeeves.

"I am," said Uncle Dudley, "a long ways from it." He always said that whether you'd heard it or not.

"Chicago—" said Mr. Liszt, "iss a dynamo. You feel it hass sometink—sometink in the air."

"It has," said Uncle Dudley, "if you live on the wrong side of town."

"New York—" began Mr. Liszt.

"What—" said Mr. Demetrios, "you do when it rains?"

"Where?" said Uncle Dudley.

Mr. Demetrios slapped his leg. He had it propped on the door of the car, his pants leg in the wind. There wasn't room for both it and the crutches in Mr. Hansen's lap. Mr. Hansen was sleepy and didn't seem to mind.

"I'd pull it in," said Uncle Dudley, "but where you think it's going to rain. Two hours we'll be in the desert—not a drop of rain."

"I like rain," said Mr. Liszt.

"Have some for you in New Orleans—nice warm rain."

"What then?" Mr. Demetrios said.

"New Orleans," said Uncle Dudley, "now there's a town."

"Too dam many niggers for me," said Jeeves. He squirmed in the seat like Mr. Liszt was one.

"Just what I like," said Uncle Dudley, "—takes a lot of them around to make up for all the white basterds I know."

"What the hell you mean?" said Jeeves.

"Basterd—" said Uncle Dudley. "Ain't you been told?" Jeeves looked all around. But there weren't any more just the same as Jeeves. He looked away and started squirming again. "Otherwise—" said Uncle Dudley, "New Orleans would be just like L.A. Full of white trash lookin for sex trash—whole goddam town a bluff. Trouble is a man never calls it—calls it romance instead. Black man tells you he wants a good woman, white man tells you he wants Love. I like a good woman more than average but I'd never find one lookin for love. I'm an old fire but the right kind of wind can still blow on me."

"For an old fire you're pretty hot," Natchez said.

"All dry heat."

"I wouldn't mind."

"That's why I would," Uncle Dudley said. Natchez looked him in the eye and Uncle Dudley looked right back.

"Ignore him," said Jeeves. "Ignore him just like me. Any man who talks niggers and against his own people is nuts."

"What you say to that?" Natchez said.

"Through teachin the alphabet," Uncle Dudley said. "Just takin on boys who read an write." Jeeves shook his head and looked at Natchez. Natchez lit a cigarette.

"You're a queer old basterd sure enough," he said. Uncle Dudley sat and grinned.

"Look at these hills," said Uncle Dudley. "Finest dam hills in the land. Some on Cape Cod like 'em— not quite so nice. Like passin your eye over a good-lookin woman—prettiest dam curves I've ever seen."

"He's got a dirty mind," said Jeeves. "That's it— a dirty mind." He looked at Natchez and Natchez grinned.

"Dam if they *ain't* like a woman—" Mr. Ahearn said. Everybody on my side looked out at them. The orange trees were sprouting new leaves, green as new grass and like Pop's cap. "I'll be damned if they ain't," Mr. Ahearn said. He looked at Uncle Dudley like he hadn't seen him before either.

"You oughta know, Red," said Uncle Dudley, and Red laughed and slapped his knee and Uncle Dudley reached and cuffed him on the back. Then they just sat and grinned at each other awhile. And right then, while it was quiet—I noticed it. The *psss-psss-psss* like a little peanut machine. But within a mile it was so loud Natchez stuck out his head to listen—he looked at me, but I shrugged like it was old stuff.

"What's that?" said Jeeves.

"Loose plug," I said. "I just cleaned the plugs." Then I pulled off the road and stopped to look at it. I fooled around trying to remember where I'd heard that noise before. Then I put the hood down and climbed back in. "Couple cracked plugs—porcelain cracked," I said. But when I put her in gear I remembered what it was. Under the pressure she sounded like a calliope. There was a town just ahead on the valley side of the road, and I turned off the motor, let her coast down.

"Gas?" said Uncle Dudley, first clearing his throat.

"Well—" I said, and looked out at the street. It was a nice clean town with big trees. There were buildings with ivy on the walls and a large open square of green grass. A young fellow with a book watched us coast by. A little farther on were stores and the P.E. tracks and I swung into the gas station on the left. I brought her up in front of two doors that said Garage.

"Five minute stop," said Uncle Dudley. "Five minutes to do it and get it done," and he smiled and slapped Red on the knee. I got out and walked into the garage. There was someone working in a pit under a Ford. Uncle Dudley came in and looked at me, lit his cigar. "Well—" he said.

"Valves," I said. "A whole dam set of valves." Uncle Dudley swallowed, then he spit. We looked out through the door at two palm trees near the tracks. There was a town in the valley and smoke rising on the sky; a P.E. car honked twice off somewhere. Uncle Dudley wiped his face with the Biltmore towel. Then he gave it to me and walked outside. I watched him lean into the car and tell Mr. Demetrios something— then lean out and tell it to Mr. Liszt. Mr. Ahearn and Mr. Hansen stood off to one side. Uncle Dudley left them there and walked to the corner where he told it to Natchez. He waited while Natchez told it to Jeeves. Then he came back and took Mr. Hansen by the arm, slapped Mr. Ahearn on his small behind. They walked across the street beneath a Coca-Cola sign.

The fellow in the pit was looking up at me. He had just had a hair cut and the sides of his head looked raw. One eye kept winking while his cigarette smoke went by.

"Hi," he said.

Right behind somewhere a noon whistle blew.

3

HIS NAME was Zeke.

He had been in the war and had a plug behind his ear which clicked when he tapped a screwdriver there. He said it sounded like a trench mortar inside. He said Marmons were really dam fine cars. All but the rear end which might go fungo any time and then where in the hell would I be? I said, caught with my pants down and he said sure. Nothing to do but just leave the dam thing there.

By four o'clock we'd done all that we could. Some of the valves were burned away and there was nothing but get new ones—Uncle Dudley phoned L.A. to send them out. That meant some time in the morning, Zeke said. He and Uncle Dudley got into the war, which Uncle Dudley said was the first, not the last—and Zeke said was both the first and the last for him. Uncle Dudley had been four months in jail instead. He said this was one country where a man could be choosy 'bout who he'd shoot—and if it was going to be lawful he'd like to start right here. He said there was more foreign basterds right in his own

43

family and why trouble to go so far to kill them off?

Zeke had to go to work on the Ford and they both went down in the pit—Uncle Dudley holding the pan to catch nuts in. Zeke said he never did warm to the French somehow. Except a little gal named Jean and that was a different thing—and Uncle Dudley said sure, that was a different thing. Uncle Dudley said the label on a woman didn't matter, all that mattered was was the contents good. Zeke said, and *how* were they good. Zeke told how he'd been gassed and woke up in a hole with the rats eating at his buddies' eyes. He'd been so weak he just lay there three days. All O.K. till he wiped his behind with a rag that still had some of the mustard gas. Some Germans came along and one was for running him through but the other one said no and won the toss. They left him with an old lady this guy knew. The old lady fixed him up and he was like a little kid only double the mess and the work she had to do. The war was over a couple months before he knew. Then he was on a boat leaving England and stretched out in a chair and when the band played the *Star-Spangled Banner* them on shore booed. He could hear them yelling Goodbye Sucker, as they drifted away. He could see their point but he couldn't see himself in another war. Uncle Dudley said they'd both live to go to jail for democracy again.

They got back to women and I came out in the sun. Mr. Demetrios was in the car eating something from a paper bag—the little man, Pop, was standing on the corner, just standing there. He was short but he was pretty broad in the beam. If something went by he kept looking at it until it was gone. His green cap sat very straight and the paper lining was still inside, tipping it up so it looked like a spade. His blue serge coat was newer than the pants and his shirt cuffs showed. He stood stiff like he didn't want to touch inside anywhere. Like he'd fallen in something and was standing up just to dry off.

I walked by and his head turned and looked at me. I walked to the corner with the bank and stood there looking at the trees. They were old pepper trees, their leaves shiny in the sun. Mr. Liszt was sitting under one, holding his hat. He saw me but pretended he didn't, looking at the sky. He kept looking at it like he saw something nobody else could see. Then he got up and walked away with very long strides. Near the P.E. station he turned to see if I was still looking— but I wasn't so he sat down under another tree. When I looked at him he turned and looked very hard at the sky.

I went in the drug store and ordered a malted milk. Mr. Ahearn and Mr. Hansen were still there. Mr. Ahearn was kidding the girl and Mr. Hansen was doing the laughing, slapping Mr. Ahearn's back with his big flat hand. Mr. Ahearn had taken his cap off to show his curly red hair which was not so crinkly as the kind showing on his chest. "Hi, Kid," he said.

"Hi," I said.

"When we gettin away?"

"Tomorrow," I said.

"Then I got all night?"

"Sure," I said.

"Well if you ain't lucky," Mr. Ahearn said, and looked at the girl. She wasn't so dumb and she'd heard all of that and looked him down. But Mr. Hansen hadn't heard it at all before and he about died. He got red and kept blowing his coffee like it was hot. When he looked up there was the mirror and he saw how red he was and blew some coffee right out of the cup. The girl didn't let on like he was red at all. She'd been around and knew different kinds—like Mr. Ahearn. I finished my malted milk and walked outside.

I went down a block, then up a wide street of trees. They were big eucalyptus trees and made an arch high over the street; way at the end the foothills were smoky blue. On one of them was a big white letter P. Schools do that sometimes and it began to look like one, a library all covered with vines and fresh cut grass. I wondered how the hell a fellow managed to go here. I walked by three girls and for the first time I saw their legs, not how Uncle Dudley would like them but how they'd suit me. They were long and coffee colored from the sun. I turned at the corner and looked back at them. One girl had good shoulders and arms, and one laughing showed her white teeth.

The others laughed and I turned and walked away. On the corner I stopped and looked down at my pants. They were new in Kansas City but not any more. My sleeves were dirty too, so I rolled them up. Two other girls came by and I crossed the street to get away, stopping to look at them from behind a tree. I took out my comb and combed my hair. In the window of a car I looked at my face—it was brown with big ears on the side—but there *was* something nice about my hair. I opened my shirt one button and pushed the tail down in my pants. Two husky fellows with blue sweaters came by. One of them had moccasins and each wore swell dirty-looking pants. "Howdy," one said.

"Howdy," I said, and walked like I had somewhere to go, past a building and between two stone gates at the end. Then I stopped like Uncle Dudley and looked around. On one gate it said that whoever went in had to keep what he came out with for everyone. I thought about that awhile and then I walked back in. I began to whistle as I walked by a swell little girl.

A wind was bending the valley smoke and turning the leaves. Mr. Liszt was not under the tree any more. From the corner by the bank I saw him cross the street and stop beside Jeeves. Natchez was standing holding his coat. He hadn't looked funny before but there was something funny now, not in any one thing he wore but all of it. Jeeves was chewing a stick of gum. His hat was pushed back and he was trying to look like Natchez, standing like Natchez with his coat off to one side. When Natchez wasn't looking Jeeves looked him up and down. Mr. Liszt pointed off at the sunset and the blue hills. When they looked Mr. Liszt turned and walked away.

Mr. Hansen and Mr. Ahearn were back in the garage. They were standing beside the Ford looking down at Uncle Dudley, Uncle Dudley still in the pit holding the pan. They were all talking about women now. Uncle Dudley was saying there was them you loved with your eyes and then there was the other kind. The other kind needn't look worth a dam but they had everything. But a man could know that and still sell himself short for his eyes. Go all out for a swell set of curves—more what men thought he had than what he got.

"Like me," said Zeke.

"And me—" said Uncle Dudley. "Man rather have a woman that looked hot stuff than one that didn't but really was. Trouble is that most men really don't know. Never havin been really taken in a man thinks the look is about all there is. Woman gets to thinkin the same dam thing. Both of them puttin up with nothin at all in order to look like they had everything. Woman takes a man that can buy her the rags and the man takes a woman that can wear them. Both of them goin short changed. Both of them cheatin at the score."

48

"Just why," said Mr. Ahearn, "I joined the navy—an just why I'm leavin it now."

"Red—you're learnin," Uncle Dudley said.

"Dam right," said Red.

I walked out and looked at the car. Mr. Demetrios and Pop were in the back. Mr. Demetrios was asleep with his leg over one of the spares, his black coat pulled up to his chin. Pop sat where his other leg would have been. He was eating a hotdog and holding a pint of milk. "How's it goin?" I said. Pop looked at Mr. Demetrios. Mr. Demetrios opened his eyes and looked at me. Grease was shiny around his mouth and there were crumbs in the hairs of his nose. "All comfy," I said. "All set for the night?" Mr. Demetrios didn't say. He made a noise with his teeth and closed his eyes. Pop took the cap off the milk and wiped the bottle top on his sleeve, then he took a very long drink. When he stopped he left the milk where it was around his mouth. He stared at Mr. Liszt, who leaned in the other side.

"You two poys slippink here?" said Mr. Liszt. The milk ran down and dripped from Pop's chin. It dripped white on his blue serge suit, his little bow tie. Mr. Liszt licked his lips and looked at me.

"There's the front," I said. "That's a big front, nice and wide." Mr. Liszt turned and looked at it. There was a hole on the driver's side but nothing stuck through.

"Efertink is a first time," said Mr. Liszt, and he

looked at me. Then he looked at Pop and Pop looked back at him. Mr. Liszt made eyes at me and I followed him into the garage. "He iss—O.K.?"

"Oh sure," I said. "Sure—"

"Slippink there?"

"He's O.K." I said. "He just don't say much—he's shy," I said.

"A for-ner?" said Mr. Liszt.

"Sure—" I said. "Maybe he don't know how." We looked back at Pop who was putting the cork on the milk. Then he stuck it into the corner of the seat. Zeke turned on the light in the garage and Uncle Dudley crawled out of the pit. Red and Mr. Hansen walked back down the street. Natchez and Jeeves moved in toward the car but Mr. Liszt with very long strides was first. He got in the front seat and looked out at them.

"What—" said Uncle Dudley to me, "what the hell's got into you?"

"Me?" I said. "Nothin—why?"

"Like hell," said Uncle Dudley. "Look at your hair—" I looked at my hair in the side of the car. It still looked all right—with a wave up toward the front.

"My hair—?" I said, surprised like.

"A buck—" said Uncle Dudley, "a regular young buck." I stood up straight and looked out through the door. By standing up straight I had an edge on my Uncle Dudley. If his hat was off I could look right over his head.

"I'm goin to college," I said. Uncle Dudley turned away. We watched a P.E. car go by and slow to a stop. Some smart-looking girls got off and walked into the light.

"Hmmmmmm—" Uncle Dudley said, and I looked back at the car. Mr. Liszt was just setting there, Pop was looking at him. "Zeke knows a place," said Uncle Dudley, "—smudging shack, couple of beds. We get a little bite to eat and go along with him." Natchez and Jeeves were standing looking at the girls. The girls walked away and Natchez and Jeeves followed them down the street. Uncle Dudley and I walked behind them toward a café. They stopped and went in, so we didn't. We walked on by.

Passage

I

THE VALVES didn't come till around five. Zeke and I worked like hell but it was eight before we topped her, everyone standing around and looking on. Uncle Dudley kept saying we'd make it up by night driving, and I let it pass just like we would. Last time he made it up at night he took the wrong road out of Phoenix—like he did the time before at Albuquerque. Then we had to make that up and somewhere near the Colorado I hit a dip going sixty-five. For two hundred miles the only thing that worked was the low gear. Then Uncle Dudley made that up by falling asleep just out of Needles and when we entered town we really did.

"Where's Red?" said Uncle Dudley. We all looked at Mr. Hansen. Mr. Hansen blushed and took off his hat. Then he put it back on and blew his nose. "Have you seen Mr. Ahearn?" said Uncle Dudley, and put his hand on Mr. Hansen's back.

"For a walk," said Mr. Hansen, and wiped his face. Uncle Dudley walked around to Zeke.

"Where do they go?" said Uncle Dudley. "Where

do the kids go around here?" Zeke wiped his hands on a rag and scratched his head.

"The wash—" he said, "college kids neck in the wash."

"The *wash?*"

"Place fulla scrub trees," said Zeke, "old roads and scrubby trees."

"Far?" said Uncle Dudley.

"Just behind the College," said Zeke. "Go up three, then keep goin right. There's an open show place when they ain't got cars. They sit on the benches when they ain't got cars."

"Hmmmmm—" Uncle Dudley said. I got in and started her up. We had to hang Mr. Demetrios' leg outside but he went right on sleeping with his head on Pop. Jeeves had bought a silk muffler and wore it like a tie, folded over like Natchez showed him how. He was smoking Helmar cigarettes like Natchez too. Natchez had a thin scar in front of his ear that didn't show unless he missed a shave. Mr. Liszt sat and blinked his red eyes. "Well—" said Uncle Dudley and he shook Zeke's hand and gave him fourteen dollars in bills. Zeke was telling me how to find the Yuma road while Uncle Dudley told him how to find us. "Larrabee—" said Uncle Dudley, "try the Larrabee Y—if we ain't there ask for Levy, Levy knows us." I backed out and Uncle Dudley waved. I went up three and over and soon we were there, a winding road only one car wide. We just moseyed along pretty slow. Here and there cars were parked and I'd stop while Uncle Dudley would stick out his head and yell *Red*. When the lights showed on them the kids inside would duck or sit up straight like Pop and stare. The girls' hands were always fussing with their hair. Natchez kept making dirty cracks and Jeeves would laugh and laugh like he'd never heard all of them before. We came to a highway and I turned and started back. Then right smack the lights were on the theatre place. One of the Greek kind with an open pit. I drove up close and turned the bright lights on. "OHHHH, RED!" Uncle Dudley yelled. Three or four kids ducked behind seats but way up in the top somebody waved. Uncle Dudley got out and walked up front. "Red," he said.

"Yeah," said Red.

"I'm sorry as hell," said Uncle Dudley, "but we gotta be gettin on. An—" he said, "I'm afraid there ain't a dam bit more room." For a while nothing happened at all. Uncle Dudley just stood there, funny looking in the light. His shadow went clear up front and fell in the pit.

"O.K.," said Red. "Dam it to hell O.K. Turn them lights off for a second an I'll be right down." I turned them off and Uncle Dudley came back to the car. Jeeves was giggling like a kid with his eye at a keyhole. "Now you can turn 'em on," said Red, and I put the dims on and we watched them come down. She was a nice-looking girl with dark brown legs.

On the bottom step he kissed her quick and left her there. Coming up to the door Natchez made a dirty crack. Jeeves was giggling when Red came alongside. "What the hell you laughin at?" said Red. Jeeves turned and looked at Natchez.

"You wanta hear an old joke?" said Natchez.

"I'd love it," said Red, and leaned on the door. Natchez looked at him and Red hitched his pants. Then he turned the knob and opened the door.

"Oh well—" said Natchez, "if you feel like that—"

"I just don't feel dirty right now," said Red. Natchez pulled the door closed and took a Helmar from Jeeves. Uncle Dudley took Red by the arm and pulled him in. Mr. Hansen slapped him on the back and squeezed his knee.

"If you wouldn't get it, why repeat it?" said Natchez. "I'll tell you when you're older sometime."

"I just been sick," said Red. "Better tell me now an not later. Couple weeks from now I'd just beat hell out of you." Natchez blew a thick smoke ring and shrugged. Up about a mile we came out on Foothill and I turned right. We began to roll and she was smooth as oil now. I kept her right where she took it easy and asked for more. You can feel all of that right through the floor. The same as I felt the whistle that night in Gallup but couldn't hear the dam thing. I laid awake half the night wondering what it was. Then in the morning I saw we'd parked behind the station and out in front a big engine sat and brewed

—you couldn't really hear it and yet it filled the air. Like Chicago late at night when no street cars were around.

"Reminds me—" said Uncle Dudley, "of leavin Omaha—don't know why it should—Omaha is all up an down. But anyhow it reminds me—" he said.

"What you know about Omaha?" said Jeeves.

"I was a kid there," said Red. "Lived on a hill steep as hell and all summer they used it for testin cars. In the winter we'd coast half a mile or more. Sometimes the new cars would stall and they'd park them right in front. We'd go down an see ourselves in the paint job and look inside. My old man worked in a streetcar barn at nights. He didn't like seein the cars around and comin home he'd spread around tacks— got so we couldn't cross the street without puttin on our shoes. After a rain there'd be big puddles of tacks down below. More I think of it more I see I had a funny old man. He put a wall up in the bathroom an the only way in was to crawl in the tub— and he had the faucet and the cork end on his side. When he wanted to be alone he'd just let the water run. He'd sit in there an read a lot of stuff by a guy named Debs. Sometimes he'd get drunk and forget about the water an dam near drown."

"My old man was a Mormon," said Jeeves. "He never got over how many women his old man had. One thing he liked about being a Mormon you couldn't do any more."

"Old Mormon lover myself," said Natchez, "—sleep better one on each side."

"Me too," said Jeeves, and giggled.

"One woman—" began Natchez.

"Ain't enough," said Jeeves. "Hell, it takes two—three, keep a man clean. I've been stuffy—" said Jeeves, "since I left Salt Lake. Hell—"

"Stop the car," said Red, "so's he can crap."

"Stop the car," said Uncle Dudley. I stopped the car.

"What the hell is this?" said Jeeves.

"Hurry up," said Uncle Dudley, "get it over with. If it won't work below at least get it off your mind. When a man thinks constipation's love—"

"*You* talkin?" said Jeeves. "You been talkin nothin else."

"My talkin," said Uncle Dudley, "—takes a detour when it's dirt. Whole point of my talkin is to drain off the dirt."

"Yeah?" said Jeeves.

"Yeah," Uncle Dudley said. "Get out and drain it off or keep on the lid." Jeeves looked all around. He looked at Natchez and Natchez winked.

"I think," said Jeeves, "I'd like my money back." Uncle Dudley crawled over Red, got out of the car. He took off Jeeves' three bags and that left the hood clean. He carried them over to the grass along the road. Jeeves finally got out. He looked at Uncle Dudley, watched him count out twenty bucks.

60

"Five dollar charge for fumigatin," Uncle Dudley said.

"What about Natchez?"

"Natchez just stinks," said Uncle Dudley, "just a plain stink. And when it gets too bad Natchez knows it, sprinkles perfume around." Natchez began to laugh. Jeeves just stood with the bills in his hand and looked at the car. Uncle Dudley told Natchez to get up front—Mr. Hansen moved back in the rear. That left just Red and Uncle Dudley on the spares—be nearly comfy now. Uncle Dudley slammed shut the door. "O.K., Kid," he said, and I started up, moved slowly by Mr. Jeeves. When I shifted to second we could hear him yell—then it was quiet, just the tires on the road. Natchez lit up a Helmar and grinned.

There was a fog in the mountains but on the other side, coming down, was a moon. The desert was like dirty snow with a lake of green ice. That was the Salton Sea. With the lights off I could really see better, see on and on up the road. It was new and lay black on the sand. Mr. Liszt was snoring little bubbles on his lip and Natchez sat and stared at the moon. Side on he was good looking—front on something went wrong. The same that went wrong with his clothes. A piece at a time it was nearly all right but all together it was wrong. Uncle Dudley slept with his head on the seat and Red's feet in his lap. Only Pop and Natchez were awake. In the rear view mirror I could see Pop's eyes when another car passed. Once I heard him drinking some milk. When I looked back Mr. Demetrios was sitting up drinking some too. I could smell salami and his mouth was greasy and pale like the moon.

2

TOWARD MORNING we stopped for coffee and gas. Mr. Demetrios and Pop stayed in the car. When we came out it was morning behind a long line of clothes and a privy, and a dog sniffed around like it was time. He did it on the gas pump and then he did it on the front wheel. It wasn't till then that I noticed the tire was flat.

The man had a tire machine and still it took more than an hour. He said the goddam tire had never been changed before. He said what the hell you do if you get a flat on the road? He looked at all of them—then he looked at me like I knew. I bought a hammer and he gave me an old tire iron he had. The sun was on the tin roof of the privy when we left.

There was a new road over the Yuma sand. The old wooden one ran alongside and looked like a fence that had blown flat—and that's what Mr. Liszt thought it was. Uncle Dudley told him how we'd first come over it. It was just one car wide and when you passed there was hell to pay. We had to let the air

out of the tires and spread our coats out on the sand—
a pair of Uncle Dudley's shorts were out there yet.
There was a time, Uncle Dudley said, when traveling was tough. Now, he said, dam near half the roads
were paved. Everybody felt better and Red began to
sing.

We had coffee again in Yuma and asked about
roads. The fellow said it was raining like hell in the
mountains and to watch the dips. He said to go to
Gila Bend and ask about Phoenix from there. A sign
on a hotel said *Free Room and Board When It Rains*
—but it looked like a bright, clear day, so we left.

The pavement ended about a half mile out of town.
It was pretty good for gravel, the washboard angling
a bit, but the best I could do was twenty-five. At the
bottom of the dips the rain had washed the sand
away, leaving the rocks like a bed of shells. Some of
them scraped the oil pan when we crawled through.
My hands got numb from the shake that came up
through the wheel and made my fingers thick like
roller skating. But all that made me feel all right
again. I looked at Uncle Dudley and he was feeling
all right too. A really good washboard road felt good
again. You finally knew you were really out and on
the go. The land around looked pretty sad, like it
was the desert's back yard, scrubby stuff and a few
boulders scattered around. For land like that I had a
game I always played. I thought of it around Roswell,

thinking of Billy the Kid—but you can play it wherever there're boulders around. It's got to be something you come on quick and go by fast. And it's got to be big enough to hide a full-grown man.

What you do is sight down the hood at some boulder you're going to pass—taking in how big it is and how far off the road. Then you look away till you're clean by. And then you look in the rear view mirror and if you see it you *got* him—and if you don't— well then, he's *got* you. The whole idea is knowing just when to look. For you can't look long and sometimes you look too late. In New Mexico Billy got me but in Arizona I got him, two to one—so you see you can get to be pretty good.

I began to sight down the hood, not being very serious, for the car was new and I had a lot to learn about a new rear view mirror. I missed the first two but caught a bit of him in the third. Mr. Liszt was beginning to wonder and looked at me. I was just getting set again when I began to feel it in the rear— there's nothing like that feeling so you don't forget it soon. I brought her up fast but not near fast enough. It went down quick under all that weight and we thumped along about fifty yards before I eased her to the side. It was on the right rear and Mr. Demetrios looked dead. I got out and walked around to look at it. The sun was warm on my back and felt pretty good. I looked at the tube all chewed to hell—yet I didn't mind. The last time I'd looked at a tube like that it was five below. I took my shirt off and looked at Uncle Dudley in the car.

"Got to pee anyhow," he said, and opened the door.

Mr. Liszt went for a walk with very long strides. Mr. Demetrios and Pop stayed in the car. Mr. Demetrios pulled up his pants so the sun was on his leg—it was white as flour and not a hair anywhere. Natchez stood in the road like he was standing on a corner, his coat hanging the same way on his arm. He kept looking up and down like things were going by. He walked to the side of the road to spit, dust his cigarette. Red, Mr. Hansen, and Uncle Dudley sat and watched.

After about an hour or so I smashed my thumb. I had to stop and walk around and Uncle Dudley rolled up his sleeves, took a tire iron, and cracked himself across the shins. Red and Mr. Hansen carried him back to a spot of shade. Red took off his shirt and after pounding the rim awhile, sat back and looked at it. There was an iron ring that snapped on to hold the tire there—like the rings that hold the glass in the goggles you buy. Only the dam ring was rusted right to the wheel. It was like it had got so hot it had melted there. We broke everything with a point and bent the screw driver to a U—then trying to straighten it Red smacked his. He didn't say anything, just stood up straight and looked around. Then

66

with all his might he heaved the hammer to hell and gone.

After a while we both went to look for it. I thought it was twenty yards past where he thought it was. Red kept seeing snakes and standing quiet to listen for rattlers until I began to hear them too. We just stood in one place and peered around. I looked back at the car and Mr. Hansen was holding the wheel —holding it up between his hands to look at it. Then he lifted it over his head and brought it down. The ring fell out and rolled across the road. Mr. Hansen pulled the tire loose with his fingers and looked inside. Red and I left the hammer there and walked on back.

We started off again about noon. Uncle Dudley looked at the sun and said it was about one. Mr. Demetrios looked at his watch and said it was noon. Uncle Dudley tried to explain. Mr. Demetrios didn't understand. Uncle Dudley used an orange for the sun and the earth was Pop's head and he showed Mr. Demetrios how it was. Mr. Demetrios didn't understand. "Where were you," said Uncle Dudley, "when you were goin west? Why was it you had to change your watch three times?" Mr. Demetrios said that going west he didn't have a watch. Uncle Dudley peeled the orange and passed it around.

Then, all of a sudden, there were clouds. The tops piled like a woman's hair, the bottoms smooth. Cloud shadows moved across the road. It was like looking up through clear water at paper boats floating there —there was a curve to the sky and the clouds followed the curve. Mr. Liszt kept shaking his head and closing his eyes. His nose was sunburned and one side of his head. "De-boo-see," he said. "It iss wot de-boo-see said."

"Who?" said Red.

"De-boo-see," said Mr. Liszt.

"Well—" said Red, "never heard of him—but what'd he say?"

"You haf not heard of De-boo-see?"

"No—" said Red. "He heard of me?"

Mr. Liszt put his head in his hands—then took one away. He looked in the rear view mirror and saw one side was red. "My—I haf a tan," he said.

The road got so it wasn't so good. The washboard went straight across and the car rattled like marbles. Where I could I drove with one wheel off in the sand. We came to a dip with thirty yards of water to the other side. While I was thinking about it I could see it rise. I took off my shoes and rolled my pants—then I had to come back and take my pants off. When I got to the middle it was above my knees and standing there I could feel it rise. There was nothing to do but try it quick or go on back. We piled all the luggage inside and Red got out and straddled the hood—when we hit the water a pile of it went over his head. For as long as I could hold my breath I thought we were done. Then I got the idea and turned so we went down stream, coming out on a stretch of sand about sixty yards below. Then we had to let the tires down to get back to the road.

Natchez' hands got sore right away and Mr. Liszt couldn't get the idea—the pump skidded sideways or bumped between his knees. Uncle Dudley got winded quick and I wasn't heavy enough. So it left a lot of pumping for Red and Mr. Hansen to do. Red's sailor suit was drying on the hood and he did his pumping in his shorts—but Mr. Hansen did all of his right in his suit. He took his hat off and put it inside but that was all. His back got so wet you could see the red stripes on his shirt right through—only when he began to dry off the stripes were there. Nobody said anything and Mr. Hansen couldn't see. He put his hat back on and got back in the car. About three o'clock Uncle Dudley's time we got under way. And then right behind a boulder a half mile away was a store. A team of mules were tied up in the shade. Their legs were still wet and covered with mud and sand. Round behind the store was a pile of junk and some not-so-bad-looking cars, some of them with air in the tires, mud on the wheels. There was a sign up saying used parts for sale. I honked the horn and finally a stringy fellow came out. He stood on the steps awhile and just looked at us. "Tow is twenty bucks," he said. "Might lose a mule, twenty bucks is cheap."

"Tow what?" said Uncle Dudley.

"You goin west?"

"We're goin east." The fellow stopped picking his nose and just stared. He looked at the wheels and then he looked back again. "How much is gas?" said Uncle Dudley.

"Sixty," he said.

"Glad we don't need it. Glad we don't need anything," said Uncle Dudley. "Get goin, Kid."

"Forty-five," said the guy.

"Get goin," said Uncle Dudley, so I did. "There's some around or he'd never thought of comin down."

"I guess we're pretty good," said Red, "—swimmin that goddam flood and foolin him. Hell—I'll bet he thinks we're Noah or someone."

"Me too," Uncle Dudley said.

"Bygod," said Red, "I'm likin this. This is the nuts. This beats the navy. Hell, I got more water back there than I did goin to Singapore."

"Sure—" said Mr. Hansen. Everybody turned and looked at him. He had cooled down some and his face wasn't so red any more. He took off his hat and looked in at the band.

"Olie—" said Uncle Dudley, "what the hell you do?"

"Do?" said Olie.

"For money—when you want money?"

"Write," said Olie.

"Write?"

70

"To my wife," Olie said.

"I'll be goddam'd," said Uncle Dudley, and looked at the sky.

"Laun-dree," said Olie. "I go—then she go. Somebody there all time." Uncle Dudley took out two White Owls and offered him one. They had to get down on the floor to light them; Uncle Dudley stayed there. Red began to sing something that was supposed to be sad. It reminded me of something else but I wasn't napping when it happened—though it wouldn't have mattered much if I had been. She blew right on a sharp turn for the tracks, but we went right by and ran alongside between two high piles of railroad ties. There was a bed put there for the ties and that was all. Then it dropped off in a gully of boulders I could look down in when we stopped. We all just sat awhile and looked out at our own dust.

"One thing about the navy," said Red. "There's room, you got plenty of room."

Nobody said anything but Uncle Dudley handed me the jack.

I had an awful time getting the thing in place. The wheel was so small it let the frame right on the ground; I had to dig a hole and drop the jack inside. Then the jack went down and the frame stayed right where it was. The place we were on was just a pile of sand. I took a floor board out of the car and just about made it before she cracked—then I took the

other one out and that one held. When I got the wheel
off I gave it to Olie again. We all stood around and
watched him pick it up. He flipped it about like a
steering wheel then lifted it and brought it down—it
stuck up in the sand right at his feet. He pulled it
out and walked back to the road. He found a nice
hard place and when it bounced the ring fell off. We
all cheered and Olie felt pretty good. But when I got
the tire back on the ring wouldn't fit. Looking at the
wheel I saw some of the spokes were loose—and on
that side the ring was a little flat. Olie had gone and
bent the dam thing. I pumped it up anyhow and the
tire spreading held the ring. I bounced it around and
it seemed all right. I put the wheel on and we all got
in. We had to wait for Mr. Liszt who had walked
away down the tracks, then he came back with some
pale little flowers, and cockle burrs in his seat. He
didn't know about the burrs till he got in and sat
down. Then he had to get out and stoop over till
Uncle Dudley was through.

I took it easy, running the front wheel in the sand.
The sun went off in a haze and everyone got drowsy;
Natchez put his coat where Mr. Liszt could sleep.
Mr. Demetrios talked about his sunburned leg. Uncle
Dudley rubbed it with oil from the five gallon can
and put some on Mr. Liszt while he was asleep. Red
put his head in Uncle Dudley's lap, hung his feet outside. Mr. Hansen dropped off just like he was. I began
to get that way myself and told Uncle Dudley to

watch me—but the next time I looked at him he was asleep. I got to playing the game of waking up just in time. Then I didn't quite and the scare woke me up good. There was a low haze—then the sky went up like on the Panhandle, up and up till it seemed the world was all sky. There was a planet right where the haze thinned clear. Beneath faint lights were blinking and smoke from a town. On the rise I shut off the engine and we coasted in. I pulled into a gas station before she stopped. There was a tinkling noise, like glass chimes, somewhere up front. I got out and walked around to see what it was. The wire spokes were just hanging there like a Chinese blind. There didn't seem to be any of them left in place. A fellow came out with a flashlight and turned it on the wheel. Then he just pushed at it—like you push a thing to see if it's there. It was there all right and then it wasn't—it started to lean. Mr. Demetrios woke up and slowly pulled in his leg.

Nobody in town had ever seen a Marmon before. One man said he just wouldn't believe it anyhow. "There's three kinds of cars now," he said. "What the hell we want with more?" It was the first time I ever saw my Uncle Dudley stumped. He stopped asking people and we went off to phone L.A.

Mr. Demetrios and Pop were asleep in the car. Mr. Demetrios hung his leg outside where it was cool. Pop slept curled in the seat with his green hat on the spare.

Natchez and Mr. Liszt were down the street in a light, looking through the window at some men playing pool. Mr. Liszt's nose looked raw and sore. He was smiling like what he saw was very funny and looking at Natchez like he thought so too. The sound of the balls was the only sound anywhere. After while a model-T backed up, started out of town. Red and Mr. Hansen looked at a horse, a brown and white pinto with a silky tail. He was tied to a buggy seat in front of the saloon. A lariat and a rifle hung from the saddle horn. Someone had whitewashed over the SALOON but it had all washed off and was SALOON again. One door had holes cut in it to spell *Café*. Red and Olie peeked over the top, then they went inside.

I waited for Uncle Dudley and we went for a walk. He was tired and kept hitting the cracks like he did when he was pooped. We had a plate of ham an', and he felt better some. He talked with a man about Steamboat Springs and what dam fine country it was —and the man told him about a place he had. Ten thousand feet and you scoop the trout out with your hands. On an old timber road just wide enough for a model-T—only you had to back in all the way it was so steep. They'd been around Lymie and down the Green River—and they liked that too. He said there was a canyon up the Snake like a hole to hell. He said it made the Grand Canyon like this dam near beer. He showed Uncle Dudley where it was and how far he'd have to walk—he didn't know about using the

74

river to get in, he said. Uncle Dudley took off his coat and the man warmed up the coffee. He set the pot on the counter and took his apron off.

I walked out past the lights and just sat awhile. The top sand was still warm but the air was cool. I lay back and it was like I'd pulled the covers up. Looking at the sky I remembered something I'd read in a book—a book about a man and a donkey traveling somewhere. Lying there, like me, he'd looked up at the sky. And he'd felt what the Boy Scouts feel first night out. After a while you don't feel that way about it any more. I wrote a paper once too but I wouldn't write one now. You have to stop looking at it to write about it at all. When you got it to look at you don't like it the other way. I looked at it then got up and walked into town.

Mr. Liszt and Natchez had gone inside. Mr. Liszt was watching Natchez chalk his cue. Nearly all of them were watching Natchez chalk his cue. The ring on his finger flashed the light around. He studied the shot awhile and then he did it the hard way—a double bank with english all the way. But he did it and turned away before it clicked. The men came over and gave Mr. Liszt the dough, each of them dropping four bits in his hand. Natchez stood and smoked letting it squint his eye. Mr. Liszt piled the silver on the edge of the table and Natchez put down the chalk, blew his fingers clean.

Red and Olie had left the saloon. Uncle Dudley

was waiting for me on a long slab of hitch stone—his shoes were off and his bare feet in the road. He had two Indian blankets, real Navajos. I carried his shoes and we walked behind the adobes, across the tracks to a warm mound of sand. We piled the top sand to a level, put the blankets down. Then we rolled over and looked up at the sky.

3

I SAT AROUND the station waiting for trains to come
in. I met a kid from Chicago going west on a
freight. He sold newspapers on the corner of Clarke
and Grand. I used to go to a movie near there and he
did too. In L.A. he sold papers on Seventh and Flower.
He said some of the people let you keep the change
around there. I'd sold papers in Omaha and knew
how it was. He said he'd been doing this for three
years now. Spring and summer in Chicago—winter
in L.A. He said he was late this year because he'd
stopped in New Orleans. In New Orleans he sold
them on Rampart and Main. We both liked New
Orleans—especially the levee there. He said he might
come around to spending the winters there. But he
said what he liked about L.A. was the babes. I told
him he ought to see the babes in a town I knew. I
told him where it was and he remembered the station
there. But he was behind the coal car and hadn't seen
much, he said. I told him in a couple years I'd be going
to school there. He said when I did to look him up—
Seventh and Flower. I said when he got back to Chi-

77

cago to look me up. I said come on around to the Y and we'll have a swim.

He came back from town with Fig Newtons and two Hershey bars. He said he usually spent about three bucks each way. I told him a car usually took about eighty-five. He said a car was a nuisance and a goddam expense besides. I said we were seeing the country, not just passing through. He said what the hell is there to see around here? I said a dam sight more than an empty refrigerator car. You tough? he said. Yes, I said, I'm tough. He tried to stare me down but I'd been through all that. Anyone who'd lived on Larrabee had been through all that. He forgot about his Fig Newtons and climbed on the freight. Then he sat down by an open ice hatch and looked at me.

"There's not a babe in town," he said, "—not a goddam babe in town."

"That's what *you* think," I said. "That's all *you* know."

He made a face but I could see he didn't know. I walked away and left his Fig Newtons there. I didn't look back till I heard her whistle and the wheels slide. When I did the Fig Newtons were gone and so was he. I watched her pull out and the brakeman in the caboose waved.

Natchez and Mr. Liszt were in front of the saloon. They were sitting on a buggy seat in the shade.

Natchez' coat was off and he was tossing quarters at a line—some of them dropped right out of sight in the dust. Mr. Liszt was dozing, his hands folded in his lap. "Pick 'em up," said Natchez, "an I'll give you one." I picked them up, thirty-one of them, and gave them to him. "Here you are," he said. "How about tossing for another one?"

"You've been practicing," I said.

"I'll put up two to your one," he said.

"O.K.," I said, and we tossed and I won. I won the next four and then we tossed for the pot. He won. I picked them up and he gave me one to play some more. I gave it back and went inside for a coke.

Red and Olie were having a coke too. There was more than a coke in Red's for it looked like weak iced tea, and Red kept looking like he was going to sing. Olie's tie was gone and his shirt unbuttoned one. But he got big so fast the second button was as tight as the first. The red stripes in his coat were pink and the sleeves had pulled up some, nearly all of his shirt cuffs hanging out. Olie's coke was darker than it should have been. He just sat and stared at the painting on the wall. A cowboy and a horse had stopped to pee in the desert and a great cloud of dust was rising up. Beneath it a sign said *What About Flood Control*. Olie didn't look very much like he got the point.

I finished my coke and walked down to the garage. Pop was sitting on the running board, shining his shoes. They were new shoes with three pairs of soles like policemen wear. They had a lining like wall paper inside. They came up to where Pop's underwear came down. His coat was off too and his brand new suspenders pulled his pants way up high like a vest. A laundry tag showed where they split in the rear. I figured Pop had had them cut off at the knees, which was why they wouldn't bend right anywhere. When he saw me he put on his coat. He walked around behind and got in the car.

Mr. Demetrios was reading the *Times*. It had been under the seat and was about eight years old, not quite old enough, Uncle Dudley had said, to be interesting. Mr. Demetrios was looking at Stocks and Bonds. He had his overcoat off but his suit coat was still on. There was a polished American Legion button in the lapel. His face was a little greasy all over now. When he turned a page he clicked his teeth and washed them around. I walked around on the opposite side but still got the smell.

Uncle Dudley didn't seem to be anywhere. I walked by the Snake River man but he was inside all alone— he was smoking and listening to a gramophone. Some cowboys were singing *Home on the Range*. When it stopped he put it back to the start again. He poured himself a black cup of coffee and sat down.

I walked out to where the old mine had been. An old timer had built a shack on the pile of slag. He was washing clothes and his underwear and his blue jeans were hung out to dry, and a shirt was spread on a cactus beside the shack. A dog and a donkey were behind in the shade. The old man looked up to watch me pass and stood ringing out his socks, then he put his hands in them and walked away. The dog got up and followed him inside.

An old hotel sat alone on the rise. It must have come before the town because it faced the wrong way, looking off like a man does, away from things. Some of the windows were out and the blinds were gone. There was a place on the side where there had been stairs but they had fallen away with the hill. I walked around to where I could see the front. It was in shadow but I could see Uncle Dudley on the porch. He was leaning on the railing and waving one arm; a woman sat and rocked in a big chair. She was dressed in black and only her ankles showed. She was big from anywhere you looked and her ankles small for how big a woman she was. Her hair was black and went back to a roll and her face was white as Mr. Demetrios' leg. She looked at me whole like Uncle Dudley did.

"Your boy?" she said.

"My brother's kid. But times," said Uncle Dudley, "I think I did the job myself." She had a fan on the floor and beside it a glass of something. She rocked all the time but somehow you didn't mind. It just made it easy to sit quiet there. I saw she wasn't white but a kind of cream color, heavy cream some places, others thin. Uncle Dudley went on where he'd left off. He said there was just one thing at his age he'd like to know. He'd like to know, he said, what she looked like when he should have met her—he knew the flower but how did she look in the bud? He couldn't remember, he said, ever having seen such a bud. In her kind the flower was ripe or no flower at all. Where had she been, he said, all the time she should have been young?

She took up the fan and it stirred the edge of her hair.

Now she was ripe, he said, and he was overdone. He wasn't sad because he couldn't remember passing her by. The thing was, where the hell was she when he did? This kid, he said, will be doing the same dam thing. Now his sap's running but he's green and before he'll see you again he'll be dry—wondering where in the hell you should have been. It's like one of us spent twenty years underground. I'm through, he said, I'm an old talk pot with no fizz, but you still owe it to the Kid. What the hell you look like when he might be passing by?

She looked at him like at a small boy that was hers. I turned and looked off at the town and way beyond. There was smoke on the sky from a train coming in from the west. I walked away and down on the road watched the train come in—watched the man unload our wheels from the baggage car. The old man who had been washing came out for his pants. He shook

82

them out in the sun and then climbed into them. I waited till I heard Uncle Dudley come walking up behind and then we went down the road toward the tracks. I had to take my hands out of my pockets to keep up.

4

"THERE'S SOMETHING dead back here," said Red. We were ready to go and I was just easing the clutch.

"What's the trouble?" said Uncle Dudley.

"Something stinks back here," said Red. Uncle Dudley thought so too but he just looked surprised. He peeked around between his legs as if it was there. "There's something dead," said Red. "Or bygod it's breathing its last," and he got out of the car and looked around. Mr. Hansen got out as if he thought so too. A breeze came along and if you hadn't smelled it before there was no chance of not smelling it now. "My gootness," said Mr. Liszt and closed his eyes. Natchez opened the door and leaned out. Uncle Dudley got out but Pop and Mr. Demetrios just sat there. Mr. Demetrios said he didn't smell *anything*. Red leaned in and said the stink was still there. The sun was very hot and whatever it was the sun made it worse. I got out and could smell it clear up front. Red said maybe it was under the seat. Mr. Demetrios complained but Red pulled till he had to get out or

84

be dumped off on the floor. Pop got up and sat on the spare. Uncle Dudley made motions with his hands and Pop sat and looked at him—Uncle Dudley reached in and took his hand and pulled him out. Mr. Demetrios leaned on the car and made a noise with his teeth. Uncle Dudley passed him a crutch but when he reached, something fell out—fell out of his other sleeve and hung down where his leg should have been. It was a piece of salami about ten inches long. One end was cut and the skin was bright and shiny with grease, but right with us all looking at it, it disappeared. It went right back up the sleeve from where it had come. Mr. Demetrios was looking us all right in the eye.

"I'm afraid," Uncle Dudley said, "I'm afraid it ain't cold enough up there."

"Suits me," said Mr. Demetrios, and clucked his teeth.

"O.K.," said Uncle Dudley. "But you're not livin alone—there's five of us sharin the room with you. You can either hang that out in the hall or spend the winter here."

"We gotta eat," said Mr. Demetrios.

"So do we," Uncle Dudley said, "and that dam meat needs an airing like you do. Hang it out. Hang it out right here," he said, —"right here alongside." Mr. Demetrios looked to see where. Uncle Dudley showed him just where it could hang, right beside Mr. Demetrios' head. Mr. Demetrios looked at Pop and Pop took out a slice of cheese. From each pocket he took out a ring of baloney, the skin tied at the cut end. Mr. Demetrios pulled on the string for salami, let it hang out in front of his vest. Uncle Dudley took it all. He wrapped it in newspapers with the bottom side open and then hung it all from the side. Mr. Demetrios held on to the paper. It kept the sun from his face and while we looked at him he began to read. We all climbed back in again. The stink was still there but seeing the reason outside made it seem not quite so bad. Even though we knew that wasn't the smell. Red leaned so far forward he could smell Natchez' hair which was something like pink candy tastes. Then we went out of town toward Ajo.

Nothing went wrong all the way. Once I stopped because I couldn't believe it and looked at the water and tires. But I didn't risk stopping again. Everybody felt good, then nobody felt right—sitting tight waiting for something to blow. When we saw smoke from the town everybody sat up like we were coming down to the finish line. When I pulled in we all were pooped. They just sat there while I got out and checked the tires and smelled the gas go pouring in. Then I got back in and started up.

"Where you headin?" said the man.

"Phoenix," Uncle Dudley said.

"Can't," he said. "The road's closed." Uncle Dudley woke up and looked at him.

86

"Just where," he said, "just where in the hell did you think we were goin?"

"Just what stirred me to askin," said the man. That woke everybody up and we all looked at him. But except for that he looked all right.

"Any other place," said Uncle Dudley, "any other roads goin anywhere?"

"There's a kind of road over the mountain," he said.

"To where?"

"Tucson," he said, "after while—"

"After while?" said Uncle Dudley.

"Yeah—after while," he said. Uncle Dudley began to breathe out loud.

"You been over it?" said Uncle Dudley.

"Never been to Tucson," he said. "Some people like it—reckon I'll go some day."

"Over that road."

"Other one likely be open by then."

"Let's go, Kid," said Uncle Dudley.

"Where's that road at?" I said.

"Only one road," he said, "you can't miss it. On the top is a tradin post for Papagos."

"He drive a car?" said Uncle Dudley.

"What'd he want with a car?" He shook his head and looked at us like we were nuts.

"Tell me—" said Uncle Dudley, leaning over confidential like, "you ever see, hear tell of, know, or read about somebody drivin it in a car?"

87

"One right here in town," he said, "dead now—fellow named Joe."

I put it in gear and we moved out in the street. "Well—" said Uncle Dudley, "do we—or do we go nuts?"

"Let's go," said Red. "Hell, let's go." Then— "What are Papy-goes?" Uncle Dudley started—then stopped. At the end of the street the road turned sharp and what looked like a cow trail began. I should have turned back but we went on. There was something horsey about all of us for nobody said anything. Nobody said anything—and then there was no place to turn. "Papy-goes," said Red, "what the hell's papy-goes?"

About a mile above the town we straddled the trail. Parts of it had been a road and there was wagon room between the boulders—but now scrubs were growing on the edge and the center was bare. The foot path was smooth and dusty with donkey manure. When we knew we should have turned back there was no chance to turn. It got dark while we sat and argued what to do. Some Indians stood off a ways and looked at us. But when I said Tucson one of them pointed up the road and we all felt better and started on again. It was soon so steep I had to shift to low. At that speed our lights were dim and flickered like a fan was turning in front—I had to stop and race the motor to see ahead. Coyotes were thick as cats behind a store.

Their eyes blinked at the lights and when we got by they sat and howled, the echoes nice but the real thing too near. There were gullies that stood us on end and bent the bumper back on the fenders, and bumps I had to squeeze around or drag the rear end. One dropped off so sharp that Red was up to his shoulders in it—all he had to do was stoop to walk under the car. That one bent up the rear fenders and broke off the spare. But the only thing that worried me was keeping her under way. The battery was running down with lights and if she stalled we were S.O.L.— I kept racing the engine like hell all of the time. But she had power to burn, even when the hood leaned up like a wall. After while I kind of liked it, kind of wanted bigger gullies to come along, liked to give her the soup and watch her climb right out. She had enough stuff in low to climb a tree. When it got really bad Red walked up front, his white cap pinned on his behind, waving one of Uncle Dudley's under-shirts at me. No telling how long they both were flat before I knew. Both of them, both of them on the rear. I didn't say anything, there being nothing really to say and no point of saying it anyhow. Funny thing was how nobody noticed it. When the road eased off and Red got back in it even seemed like she ran pretty smooth, which showed how it was back where we'd come from. We rolled along in second and it felt like high. Only when a light appeared, and then the moon, did I feel Uncle Dudley looking at me—nobody else

89

noticed the tires at all. Not until the last rise and we could see the tin roof of a building—when the left front went and I couldn't keep her in the road. But she pointed right for the building so I let her go. And they all just sat and looked while we bowled over cactus and scraped rocks along, then all at once it was smooth and we stopped in the yard.

5

HIS NAME was O'Toole—call me Jerry, he said. Uncle Dudley did right off the bat and he called Uncle Dudley Willie—called him that without ever asking his name. They stood slapping and cuffing each other like they were old friends. He was older than Uncle Dudley and half again as fat, his face round and the color of black walnut stain. The top of his head was bald but around the sides was fluffy white hair. It made him look like a chocolate egg in a cotton nest. The rest of us just sat and watched the two of them carry on. They got to laughing so hard they could hardly stand, stopping just long enough to listen to each other's jokes. Finally they took a breather and both looked in at us. "Welcome to Valhalla!" Mr. O'Toole said, and then they laughed and laughed again, the rest of us just sitting and looking on.

"Goddam if I see what's so funny," said Red. That made them even worse, and Mr. O'Toole had to sit down.

"Valhalla?" said Mr. Liszt.

"Goddam if I get it at all," said Red. We sat a-

while and listened to them laugh. I got out and looked
at the tires. They were still on but a brand new way,
the bead just folded around the edge of the wheel. The
rim had cut through in places but not all the way.
The wheel just flapped around loose in the casing,
rolling over on it rather than with it, the top of the
tire baggy and loose. It was an idea—a good idea for
roads like this.

They all sat inside until Uncle Dudley and Jerry
walked away. Then Red and Olie got out, and after
a while Mr. Liszt and Natchez. They walked around
like people just off a train. Mr. Demetrios reached
and pulled his salami in. The moon was bright on the
roof of the store and you could read the tin signs on
the front. Chew Mail Pouch and Gorton's Cod Fish,
they said. The building was like a model-T with a
hump in one end. There was one window smack in
the middle of one side. We could hear Uncle Dudley
laughing and one of them slapping the counter, then
they came out with a load of stuff and built a fire.
There were boxes around and they pulled one up and
sat down. They were both having so much fun it
gave you a pain. We all stood off and watched them
but they didn't mind, they seemed to forget that we'd
come along, carrying on like a couple of Boy Scouts.
Mr. O'Toole began to cook some kind of meat. He
held it over the fire on a stick and when the smell got
around Red and Olie moved in—Red pulled up a
pop case and they both sat down. I did too—but they

still gave me a pain. Finally Natchez and Mr. Liszt came in and stood around. They waited for someone to say sit down, but when nobody did they just did by themselves—squatting on a board that was stretched out on the ground. But when the meat was done Jerry O'Toole served them first. Then Olie, Red and me, with Uncle Dudley passing sardines. Before we knew it, it was a picnic, everybody feeling pretty good again, moving away when the fire got hot— then moving in. For dessert we had dried apricots and strawberry pop. Strawberry, he said, was the only color he had. He said the Indians bought it by color and they liked this color best—this color spiking pretty well too, he said. He had his own teeth and they were bright as light in his face. He had an old Hopi ring with silver rain drops and the turquoise looked like it should on his hand. It was thin and old like an Indian's, the fingers long.

He said we were the first white meat he'd seen in a week of moons. He said before the war he was going to die and the doctors gave him a year to live, and he spent six months of it just mooning around. He got to seeing what they did with dead people and it made him sick. So he got a grub stake and a donkey and left Denver in the spring. He got back in here the following winter he said. He thought it was a dam swell place to die and paid an Indian to cover him with rocks—then he just sat around awhile and waited for it. First thing he knew he ran out of grub and hadn't died. He didn't want to buy grub and waste it—so he opened the store. The building was here when he came, used to be a pack stop to Tucson. Before he knew it he had to remind himself he was going to die. Then it was too much trouble and he just said to hell with it. He didn't know till '24 that America had been in the war—another guy came up to die and mentioned it. He didn't die either but he got bored and went home. Twice a year a fellow came up from Tucson to do some sleeping and a little hunting, otherwise he didn't see any white meat at all. He'd taught a Papago squaw to read English just so he'd hear it once in awhile—but she could only read one story and she knew it by heart. For all he knew she couldn't read but just learned it that way. He had some stories of Conrad and he'd taught her "Typhoon." About a year ago she'd died and he thought he'd have to read to himself, when he found her boy knew the thing by heart. He'd learned it just sitting around listening to her. For a bottle of strawberry pop he could have a Typhoon at any time.

Mr. Hansen wanted another bottle of pop. Must be some Indian in him, said Jerry O'Toole, and they all laughed but Olie. Then when they stopped he began to laugh too.

"My wife like it too," he said, and looked very happy. He started to say more but it caught some place, came out like water in his eyes. He held a piece of wood to protect his finger and opened the strawberry pop with his thumb. He shook it up to make it fizz and took a drink.

"Bygod—" said Red. "If a man had a woman— a dam good woman—I'd like it here. No crap or noise or dirt around. Hell, it's like living on the goddam moon." We all looked at it, so bright it jittered some.

"No—" said Mr. O'Toole, "you got to like it alone. When you say woman you said too much. You're expecting her to be everything you left behind—instead of leaving it you try to bring it along. While your blood is hot you don't want to live up here. When it cools you may want to even less."

"I'm coolin—" said Uncle Dudley, "but it wouldn't suit me. Ain't that I don't like it—but I know myself too well. Now and again I like to find some people around. And by now and again I mean hell of a lot more than twice a year. Half what I like is that I know I'll be movin on. This all seem even better to me rememberin it in Lincoln Park."

"I don't know," said Jerry O'Toole, "why I like it here. I don't even know if I like it or not. I stopped thinking that way when I stopped waiting to die. I just live here like I lived other places before. If you get along you don't ask why you're living there. It's the strangers that ask it—people just passin through. I sit and look at nothing now like I used to look at them—at the sky like I did the passin cars. I'm not sure I see any more or any less. When a man gets along his eyes turn in anyhow. Sittin here I can turn them

95

in or out by myself. Maybe that's what I like about it
—if I like it here."

"It iss the lant," said Mr. Liszt, "the lant and the
sky. Here a man hass a spirit—here a man hass a
soul—" He looked all around at them and his eyes
were wet. He and Mr. Hansen looked at each other a
long time. Then Mr. Hansen sighed and made more
fizz.

"Well—" said Mr. O'Toole, "what I once thought
myself. Now I know it's a lot of sentimental crap.
Spoils a man a long time before he gets over it. People
born and raised out here have no more soul than the
rest, fact is they have even less. This soul stuff is a
lot of gook spread on a man before he's learned to
wash himself. Out here there's some chance of being
washed clean. Whatever you are at bottom you get to
be more everyday. Take an Indian now. There's some
fine talk spread around about what a soul he has. But
it isn't so much what soul he has but what soul he
hasn't. Until we rub him with our kind, then he gets
that too. Soul is the soft spot in a man that'll take all
the salve we can give it. The Indian's a man and he's
got a soft spot too. But his own Great Spirit isn't
that kind. If a tree could pray he'd ask for sun and
rain and fruitful seeds—and that's what an Indian
asks for, and all he needs. He's like something that
grows out here—then he's like us. Cut him off, give
him a soul—and you've got a potted plant. Open the
window to one of *our* storms and he'll blow clean

to hell. Same storm that blows some of you pale face seeds out here."

Mr. Liszt didn't quite get it all—but he got the idea. He looked across at Mr. Hansen shaking his bottle again. But all of the fizz was used up now and didn't *pssss* on his thumb. He held it up to the fire and looked at it.

Uncle Dudley lit a White Owl and rocked on his seat. I began to see now why he just smoked and sat by. It was like hearing himself talk without troubling to. Being able to sit and enjoy it at the same time.

"Don't know a goddam thing about Indians," said Red, "but no soul stuff for me. A man's a man or he's just some rundown heel. I suppose some are half an half but I just don't know. What I've seen is one or the other and all the way." Mr. O'Toole nodded—but he didn't say anything. That left it up to Uncle Dudley and he cleared his throat.

"Hard to know what a man is—but I know what I like. Two kinds I like. I like the big fella you can't keep down and the little guy you can't keep up. Maybe I like the little guy even more. He's as far below average as the big fella is above, but he's alive —an the average guy is dead. If we're ever a country of average guys we're all dead. Average guy can't fail any more than the little guy can succeed—ain't why I like him but why I like him so much. Point is, he fails for better reasons than he succeeds. He fails because he's not a shrewd basterd—just a little guy. He ain't

97

even shrewd enough to look like what he ain't. I don't like him because he's down but because his being down makes sense. He's there for reasons that make him the better man. And when he stops failing for those reasons, bygod we've all failed. He's the one that believes what should be true and buys bargain socks without any heels—on Sunday his new shoes squeak louder than the choir. He looks like the man in your mother's album, still wearin the same collar and tie, the man she didn't pick but sometimes wished she had. And we die laughin how funny he looks, like at another funny little man. And like we die laughin at Charlie, there's a lump that's tryin to cry. Maybe I think this little guy plays the biggest part. The big fella's here to ask what the fires are but who the hell's going to keep them burning? I don't know who if it ain't the little guy—"

Mr. Hansen poured the rest of the pop on the ground. Mr. O'Toole looked at Uncle Dudley something like the big woman did. Uncle Dudley fiddled with his cigar. "I know," said Red, "dam well I'm not a big fella—yet I wouldn't say the little guy's what I thought I was."

"You're a nobody guy with somebody's guts," Uncle Dudley said.

"That's like it," said Red. "That's something like I think."

"What am I?" Natchez said. Uncle Dudley was

surprised but he didn't let on. He struck a match but his cigar was still lit.

"Think I already told you," he said.

"Pretty well—" Natchez said.

"You're a kind of a shame," said Uncle Dudley. "For you got something on the ball. But somewhere you got to thinkin that puttin it on the ball was enough." They looked at each other and Natchez grinned. "Time being," said Uncle Dudley, "you're what Red calls a heel."

"Right on the head," said Red. "He ain't as bad as that Jeeves stink pot but it's the same smell." Natchez made a great yawn. "But don't know but what I think this air's helpin," said Red. "Don't notice it half so bad—"

"Marked that myself," Uncle Dudley said. "Course there's more room out here—have to get right close to any smell."

"You brave little men hurt me no end," said Natchez. "Mind my leavin your council of war?" He stood up and stretched his arms. But Mr. O'Toole threw on another log—after a moment Natchez sat down again. The fire was bright on the side of the building, the front half was like a hive of small holes. Uncle Dudley saw them and got up to look closer, felt some of them with his hand.

"You had a war up here?"

"Every full moon," said Mr. O'Toole, "—a war and a peace at the same time. When the boys are full of

99

fire water we have the war—peace is they just use the front end. That and no war until the lights are out. Way back somewhere they had a war with this building and they're slow to change their ways. Don't mind any more except the sometimes I forget. Walk out here in the yard and some young buck shoots the buttons off me."

"Just full moons?"

"So far," he said. "Somebody brings the moonshine up from below and they have a dance—then they have a war. Sometimes they get to crackin away from both sides. Couple of them been hit but nobody died as yet."

"You call that a full moon?" said Red. We all looked at it but it wasn't quite.

"No," he said. "But if I was pretty well cocked I might. Nights like this I just pretend it is." We all turned and looked back at the rise. The rock slabs were bright and the cactus was alive. "Haven't heard anything—but I wouldn't wander around."

"I won't," said Uncle Dudley. They looked at each other and began to laugh again. Red looked at me and I looked at Red but we weren't sure if it was kidding or not. From behind Mr. Liszt Pop walked into the light. He walked up to the fire and held out his hands. There were creases in his pants and he smoothed at them, then he brushed the dust from a spot on his sleeve. He put his hands out again, palms down, like a little boy.

"Reminds me," said Red, "—when I was a kid. Used to have fires in the back yard all the time. Then one summer they paved the alley an the yard was fulla sand. I remember cause a kid I knew lost a chameleon there. Ever try to find a chameleon in a pile of sand? Anyhow when the alley was paved it wasn't a back yard any more. Couldn't do a dam thing, got to be like the front yard was. Women came out and emptied the garbage and stood around holding the pan. That was all that ever happened there. It was pavin that alley that made me a man before my time. Got to kissin a little Polack girl that lived next door. Spent all my time doin that or beatin up somebody that wanted to. When I saw her once after bein away she had a husband an two kids. She was out in the back hangin up diapers on the line. But she looked just the same and I walked up and kissed her right there. She dropped the clothespins on my feet and kissed me back. Right there in the goddam yard. I could see she felt it the same as me so it was up to me —and I kissed her again. Then I walked out in the alley and began to run. We hadn't said a goddam word. Up on the corner I passed a truck and I waved at him and he took me in—it was a gas truck but he let me smoke. He was a swell, knowin kind of guy."

"I suppose your heart was broke," Natchez said.

"Yeah," said Red, "—but not my head. I still kiss a woman same as I kissed her. My head is in it and not standin off lookin on. Must be hard on a woman to be

lovin a man who's his own peepin tom." Natchez
only grinned and tossed stones at the fire. Pop turned
his back and his pants began to smoke.

"In Vienna—it iss dif-runt," said Mr. Liszt.

"You don't kiss them?" said Red. Mr. Liszt wet
his lips.

"Plenty kissing," he said, "—dif-runt the way it
goes about. A poy meets a girl—they like each odder
—they go to hotel. Since the war nopody is married
any more. The poy hass no chob—the girl no dowry.
They must chust be poy an girl a lonk, lonk time."

"Suits me," said Natchez, "—think I could make a
living there?"

"Sure," said Red. "A first-rate heel gets by anywhere—only the second-rate heels got anything to
worry about."

"I'd better remind you," said Natchez, "—there's
just so much of your sass."

"Then I suppose you're gonna be a brave man,"
said Red. "I suppose you're gonna stand up and roll
your sleeves and fold your coat. Well—I'm about as
worried about your doin that as I would be if you
did." Pop felt his pants and then smelled the fingers
on that hand. He walked away without turning or
looking around. We watched his green hat go back
and get in the car.

"I was plumber—" said Olie, "then come Dee-
troit." We all looked at him. Then we looked away

but it was already too late. Olie picked up the bottle and sat and stared at it.

"Plumbing nice," said Uncle Dudley. "But laundry business even nicer. Plumbing gets everything dirty—laundry cleans it all up. Detroit's the kind of town needs a good laundry around." Olie turned the bottle upside down. He let it drip in the sand, watched the dark spot come—watched it go.

"Funniest thing—" said Uncle Dudley, "funniest and saddest dam thing I know—is how a man can't pick himself up without lettin himself down. None of us ever get any bigger than the troubles we have. An a country depends on them same dam troubles too. We're goin to get around to takin away the kind of trouble that untroubles a man—believin like we all want to believe that troubles should go. You got to be mighty smart to know what trouble to take away. Nobody makin a law will do it—nobody settin things free. For there's no one thing to untrouble all the people at any one time. There's no one thing to cover the people at any one time. There's not even any one dream for the people, or any sun or one moon for the people, for any kind of people at all there isn't even one sky. But I'll tell you one thing about the people, this is their land. And the more I see of them the less I want to cover them at all. Hell, there's no need to cover the people—they cover themselves."

"The peeple soul—" began Mr. Liszt.

"I guess what they are includes all that there is.

And when I find a piece of them I believe it—just in so far as it's them I believe it—when it's what someone wants them to be I don't believe it at all. If you're lookin for somethin they got it—when you need it it's there. Once was a time I thought I could show them where to go. Thought I was meant to ride up front and holler and point at the promised land— guess I still holler and point but I give up tryin to ride. . . ."

"I was meanin to ask," said Red, "—what the hell you thought you were."

"I'm the horseless knight," said Uncle Dudley, and he looked across at Mr. O'Toole. "I got all the armor but I can't get on a horse. And all of that armor shows I really ain't a brave man. I've learned how to think being brave isn't so smart. You got guts, Red—but I couldn't say you were brave. Brave is knowing what the hell guts is for. Sometimes it's braver to act like you ain't got any guts at all. That kind of brave ain't yet part of you. Like your kind of guts ain't yet part of me."

"I can't say," said Red, "that I seen a lot of brave men."

"I can't say I ever really seen one. I don't say they ain't—I just say I ain't been there. I always been where he was just when he got away—or didn't get away and wasn't any more. That kind of brave is my kind of man on a horse. Sometimes I think I'm that kind of brave but when I'm there it just poops out—

it just looks dumb instead of brave any more. But maybe my man with your kind of guts would change my mind. I wouldn't know till I stood alongside and seen him ride."

"I'm a horseless knight too," said O'Toole, "—but I did so much walkin my soles worn thin—I come to doubt there even horses any more."

"Bygod—" said Red.

"What haf you for aranchments?" said Mr. Liszt. Mr. O'Toole took out his pipe and looked at him.

"Do it anywhere," said Mr. O'Toole, "just don't wander around in the light." Mr. Liszt didn't understand.

"He's been—" said Natchez, "just wonders where to sleep." Mr. O'Toole got up and went inside. He came out with an armful of blankets, dropped them on the ground.

"Anywhere you like—providing you don't walk in your sleep. Nothing these boys like better than something that really moves." Mr. Liszt picked a blanket up—started off. Then he came back and looked at Natchez.

"Who iss slippy?" he said. Natchez shook his head. Mr. Liszt looked at Olie but he was still busy with the bottle, filling it up slow with bits of sand.

"Nopody slippy?" said Mr. Liszt. Natchez changed his mind. He took a blanket and made a big yawn.

"There's a ridge behind," said Mr. O'Toole. "Nice warm sand but a heavy dew. Better take off your pants or they'll look like hell." Mr. Liszt pants already looked like hell. He smoothed at them in a funny nervous way. Like boys do before they get used to buttoning up. Natchez still looked O.K. Somehow his pants didn't get so wrinkled and his coat still hung straight. But his face looked tired and sad. Mr. Liszt was like something on a Xmas card. His whole face was red and when you looked at him he smiled—he smiled now but stopped because his lips were chapped. Natchez led off and they went up behind. They went up the rise and were on the sky, dark against the tin roof. Then they dropped down somewhere out of sight.

"Why I keep pickin on him?" said Red. "He ain't such a bad heel. He can be kinda nice—look at him walkin off with soulful like that. I just seem to give him hell for all the heels I ever seen. Never really took time before to tell 'em just what I thought." Olie stopped playing with the bottle and looked around. Red picked up a blanket and tossed it to him, then picked up one for himself. They went beyond the car to a slab bright with the moon. They put one down to lie on and pulled the other one up.

I got up and walked off like I had business to do. Someone was snoring in the car when I went by. The breeze was my way and the salami followed me up the rise. When I turned I could see the car and the bright roof on the store, the fire like warm cracks in the yard. It looked like a picture I'd seen at the

Biltmore. Only there weren't any white-faced steers or cowboys around. Nobody lighting a smoke with the glow on his face. And Uncle Dudley wasn't around to laugh. I watched them get up from the fire and walk into the light, Mr. O'Toole's hair like a sugared doughnut on his head. They went inside and lit the oil lamp. Mr. O'Toole went away, then was right back with a bottle—from a shelf he handed Uncle Dudley a pack of cards. Uncle Dudley shuffled them his tricky way and licked his thumb. Mr. O'Toole sniffed at the cork and then he poured.

6

I WOKE UP. It was light but still a green color, like there were too many moons. The blanket felt like wet grass. I turned away from the glow in the sky and then I heard the noise again. I raised up on one arm and looked below. Mr. Demetrios was standing beside the car. He let the door hang loose and came toward me with long easy swings. Just below he stopped. Leaning on a boulder he took off his overcoat, began to unbutton his suit coat too. Just before he took it off he looked around. Then he did and the shirt came with it, everything but the collar and the cuffs. He was the damdest looking thing I'd ever seen. The color of bones and no thicker anywhere. His cuffs hung down on strings fastened to his vest and his bag of money swung free when he stooped. I lay back and closed my eyes. I began to think of Lon Chaney in the *Phantom of the Opera* and on my arms I could feel the goose pimples come. When I looked again he was just standing there. He didn't seem to get cold, just seemed to like standing there. Then he pulled up his suspenders and looked around. He put everything on like at first and took off his hat. He wiped it clean on the back of his sleeve, set it on his head. Then he swung back to the car, let himself inside. After while he pulled the salami in.

When I looked again there was a fire in the yard. The sun was up but there was still a bite in the air. Mr. Liszt was up and walking around, Red and Olie were sitting by the fire. Mr. Liszt wasn't using long strides but he still walked with his hands behind, his coat out so it hung like a droopy tail. Pop stood in front of the car, looking at the fire. His arms were in back too and looked too short to reach his pants. When he forgot and let them hang it was all right until he saw them—then he'd quick put them in back again. He took off his cap and pushed the paper lining around. Then he sat it on very straight and looked at his pants. There was nearly a bend now where they went around his knee but they still seemed to be pushing from behind. He had to bend a little bit to look at his shoes. There was dirt caked to the bottom and he tapped one on the tire, a flat tire on the right front. I remembered it was the *left* front that went last. So that made all of them flat, four flats and three spares. I laid back until I noticed the bacon smell.

Bacon and sardines are not as bad as you think. I sat eating mine and wondering about the tires. Uncle Dudley and Mr. O'Toole had played strip poker all night and Mr. O'Toole was wearing Uncle Dudley's knickers. Uncle Dudley was walking around in his B.V.D.'s. Mr. O'Toole said he'd never tried a pair before and dam'd if he didn't think they were O.K. Only trouble was they wouldn't go around. He gave Uncle Dudley his size and made him swear to send him a pair—an Indian would pick them up for a bottle of pop, he said.

It was all pretty funny all right—except the tires. I asked Mr. O'Toole about the road and he said just to forget about it—since there wasn't one, wasn't that smartest? he said. Uncle Dudley thought that was funny as hell. There's a road till this ends, he said, and from there you can see Tucson—you can pick your own for the next thirty miles. The way they all laughed you'd think they were living here. They began to play poker again before they'd even licked their fingers, and on the first hand Uncle Dudley won back his pants.

I decided to hell with it. I jacked up a wheel at a time and squeezed on one of the spares, making a cushion of two flats on each one. The right front had to ride as it was. I made holes along the bead and wired the outside tire to the wheel, because it spread a little too wide to ride on its own. But it left the front end dam near the ground. If going down was like coming up it was all off. When I got back and looked at her she looked more like a sled—the wheels like a kind of snowshoe you put on. But she had rolled up—so she might roll down. I walked back and looked at the poker game.

Red and Olie were already sunburned. Olie had his hat but Red was stripped to the waist, and a fellow that freckles doesn't tan any too well. Natchez was wearing all but Olie's hat. They were piled high with Red's sailor bonnet on top and Natchez was smoking a White Owl cigar. He didn't look tired or sad any more—he just looked good.

"O.K.," I said. "Time we're gettin along."

"One hand of pot luck," said Uncle Dudley, "the whole works in the pot." And I was standing right behind Natchez and watched Red deal him a flush. From the pile Natchez took Red's hat—nothing more.

"I'm so sick of that thing," he said, "I'm going to put it out of circulation." And he walked over and tossed it on the fire. "Without that hat," he said, "might be able to look at you." Then he walked off without staying to watch it burn.

Red got up and left his stuff in the pile. He got in the car just as he was, stripped to the waist. Uncle Dudley brought his shirt along and tossed it to him— Red tossed it back in the yard. Uncle Dudley picked it up for him again. "Be mad," he said, "but don't be a goddam'd twirp—maybe I was wrong about what kind of guts you had. It takes more guts to take it, kid, than to give it out. Natchez dished it out this time—you want your shirt?" Red took it and put it on. He was a kid like me all right and I could see he could dam near cry. But he was some better than me because he didn't, he swallowed it down.

Mr. O'Toole gave us some more sardines and pop. He didn't look at Uncle Dudley and Uncle Dudley kept talking loud, until I started up and we creaked away. Then I thought maybe Uncle Dudley would cry. He bounced around on the seat without looking or asking why—till we came to a pass and the open slope beyond. "Hell, Kid," he said, "ain't you runnin on a flat?"

"Four of them," I said, and then he woke up and was all right.

There she was. Like the down side of a wave the slope was smooth and clean, a spot like smudge on the sky over Tucson. No road anywhere and not much need of one. Most of the shrub was so low it just brushed underneath, and we followed the streams until there was a chance to cross. The sand was firm and smooth as a road. Sometimes soft—and then it was nice to have flats, the tire spreading wide on the crisp top. It got pretty hot but that was all. Once we followed a stream in the wrong direction but that was all right because we got a bath. Cold as hell, but even Red felt good. About three o'clock we came out in the flat and followed a wire fence east to the road. There the fence went north without a gate. Red, Olie and I took some of it down. I loosened the poles with the car and then Olie pulled them out, holding the fence on its face till I got by. Then we followed the ditch till we could make the road. A road grader was working and he stopped to watch us go by. We didn't say anything. We just went by.

The first cop in Tucson picked us up. It wasn't hard—all he had to do was walk along side. He walked along side clean through town to a place outside. Then he asked Uncle Dudley who the hell he thought he was. Uncle Dudley opened the door and got out of the car. He didn't say anything to the cop, just turned and looked at us. "You'll pardon me a moment?" he said.

"Yes sir," I said. "Yes sir—"

Then he walked past the cop and right in the station door. The cop just stood and wondered what the hell. He came back and looked at us, then he walked and peeked in the door—he was still peeking when Uncle Dudley came out. The Chief was along with him, red in the face. He stopped and stared, shaking his head like he couldn't believe it, then he looked at Uncle Dudley like *he* was Chief. "I tell you, sir," he said, "can't blame Grady much for this—that's a piece of camoflagin that might even fool me!" Uncle Dudley just shrugged and smiled. The Chief came and looked inside, first taking off his hat, shaking hands with Mr. Hansen and Natchez. "Only thing I notice," he said, turning back to Uncle Dudley, "is maybe you overdone it a bit." Uncle Dudley looked at all of us again.

"Best types I could find," he said. "All modeled on life itself. Isn't Mr. Blake a crook if you ever saw one?"

"Bygod—" said the Chief. "Bygod, he really is."

"Well—" said Uncle Dudley.

"Very sorry," said the Chief. "Really very sorry, but I think that Grady—"

"Of course," said Uncle Dudley, "matter of duty, should be congratulated." He turned and smiled at Mr. Grady. Mr. Grady stared. "But as you say—it *is* a little overdone. Will pick up some tires here, soften things down a bit."

"Just a little," said the Chief.

"You've a good eye," said Uncle Dudley. The Chief smiled, looked at Mr. Grady.

"Perhaps an escort?" he said.

"Give us away?" said Uncle Dudley.

"Of course," said the Chief. "Foolish of me. Well—"

"Well—" said Uncle Dudley.

"If we can be of any service—anything at all—"

"Glad to call on you," said Uncle Dudley. "Meanwhile—better pick up some tires. Some place near here, dependable, discreet?"

"Grady—" said the Chief, "take them down to Miller's." Grady nodded his head.

"Well—" said the Chief.

"*Adios!*" said Uncle Dudley.

"*Adios*," he said.

Grady walked along side and we went back into town. Uncle Dudley didn't say anything, he just looked sad. From a block away Grady pointed at Miller's, a sign bright in the sun. Then he backed away and watched us crawl along. When we got to Miller's, I turned in and we went right out the other side—the doors open and nobody standing around. Down the block was a little dump saying TIRES. I stopped and Uncle Dudley went in. We watched him talk to a man inside and saw the man come and stare from the window, looking at Uncle Dudley, then back at us. Then Uncle Dudley came out and leaned in the car. "I'll have to have some dough, boys," he said, "anything you can spare—whatever you got." Red and Olie right off gave him five apiece. Natchez gave him three. Mr. Liszt after feeling around finally found two. Uncle Dudley took the fifteen and went back inside. The doors opened and the man waved at me to come on in.

"Your Uncle," said Red, "is the goddamdest man I ever seen."

7

IT WENT so good nobody said anything. Before midnight we were in Bisbee, winding down into the lights, something like coming into Trinidad. It was like a piece of the sky upside down. I waited for Uncle Dudley to say so but he just sat quiet; he didn't even smoke to break the spell. We had coffee and still nobody said anything. Everybody looked up and down the counter like a secret was around, everybody in on it but nobody willing to tell. The waitress chewed her gum and looked at Red. Red didn't even so much as ogle her. Mr. Liszt got out a map and we all looked at it, seeing how far it was to El Paso, New Orleans. But nobody really figured how far it was. And nobody made any guesses out loud. We stood on the curb awhile and picked our teeth. The lights went up from the street like a stairway, mixed in with the stars. There was the same funny, silent whistle around. Like a leak in the earth somewhere—or a kettle on. Mr. Demetrios was asleep with his leg hooked over the crutches and everybody had to climb in the other door. As we coasted away Red began to sing.

After Douglas I took it for granted too. The road went north in long slides, most of them dropping down—you couldn't see it but I could feel it through the floor. The same gas good for sixty instead of forty-five. They were talking about women when we crossed the state line and only Uncle Dudley saw what it was. He just tapped me and said—"Kid, you awake?" When the moon came up I could see the shape to the land. Sprawly country, where a mile looked eighty yards, snow on the high range north and west. The road went along between two big mesas, the land sucked up like the sides of a wave. Beyond it began to level some. After Deming there was just the sky and the telephone poles. The gravel was a thin ripple board, smooth at forty-five. I drove down the middle to give me leeway when I dozed. And somehow I must have been dozing during the fight. First thing I knew Uncle Dudley was saying to stop the car. I said what—and he said to stop the car. I pulled up to the side where a pile of gravel was stacked, I figured it was just that somebody had to go. But when I stopped nobody moved. I heard Uncle Dudley fishing around and thinking it was for paper I handed him some. "Sorry, Kid," he said, "but it won't wipe up what I got in mind." Then he pulled the handle out of the jack and got outside. "You're a big basterd," he said to Natchez, "or I'd figure on using my hands—but I ain't so wiry any more. Which you pick," he said, "the handle or the jack?"

"Why you goddam old fool," said Red. "Get back in here—Natchez is mine," and he started to back out of the car. Uncle Dudley caught him stooped with a full swing of his leg and Red spread out flat on the two spares.

"Both you kids think I'm kiddin—an both of you are goin to be cured." Uncle Dudley turned back to Natchez again. "O.K.," he said. "Which you pick?"

"Get back in the car, old man," said Natchez, "—no point in me callin your bluff." He was grinning a little when Uncle Dudley slapped him full. Right flat across the mouth and it jarred his hat clean from his head—he put his hand up and when he took it away it was red. He gave his hat to Mr. Liszt and got out of the car. Uncle Dudley held out the parts and Natchez took the piece with the head. Uncle Dudley took the handle and dropped the rest inside. Neither of them looked drunk, I couldn't smell anything. I looked at Red and Olie and they weren't drunk, yet they were all nuts. Uncle Dudley walked out and stood in the lights. He rolled up his sleeves and looked so funny standing there all I could do was swallow and blink my eyes. Natchez walked out and was a half head taller—he just looked sad.

"O.K., Kid—" said Uncle Dudley. "You honk the horn and we start to swing." He looked at me and I didn't do anything. I sat and stared till they both blurred over and my eyes burned. "Honk that dam horn," yelled Uncle Dudley. "Red—lean over and

118

honk that horn." I felt Red lean on me and I scrambled to cover the wheel. But with all the messing I set off and I think I yelled and closed my eyes—but when nothing happened I looked. Uncle Dudley was standing out there alone. He wasn't looking at anything on the ground but off somewhere across the road. He walked out of the lights to look for it better, looked at the moon. There was a fence edging the road and behind it a desert of shrubs. Ahead in the lights some Herefords lined up and stared. Uncle Dudley came back and stood in the light. "Oh Natchez!" he yelled. "Come on out here or be left bygod!" Nothing sounded anywhere. Some of the steers wandered down our way and stopped right along side. In the moonlight their eyes were like knot holes in a white fence. "Last call," said Uncle Dudley, "I'm gettin cold standin here." It all seemed pretty dam funny now, we could even laugh. Uncle Dudley stooped over and picked up the jack head where it had dropped. He brought both pieces back and stood unrolling his sleeves. He took Natchez' coat and hat and unroped his bag from the side. He put them all up front in the lights, came back to the car. "Fact is, Natchez," he said, "I had something like this in mind. But you've gone it too far—you're leavin it right where it was." A steer scratched himself on the fence somewhere. "Well—" said Uncle Dudley, "last call!" Then he came and got in. We waited awhile and then he said, "O.K., Kid." I let her just crawl for a block or so.

After that there were no more steers and the land looked empty again; you couldn't believe there was really somebody there. About five minutes ahead the lights of Lordsburg showed. Getting gas Uncle Dudley told the fellow about a man we'd passed—nice-lookin guy, Uncle Dudley said, but we ain't got room. Likely pay for a ride into town, he said, likely pay pretty good. While we were pulling out the fellow was cranking his Ford. A red lantern hung on the rear and went back down the road.

The gravel had just been scraped and the only noise was the wind. Mr. Liszt just sat and stared at the road. He had the whole seat now to himself and seemed a little lost, just sitting quiet between me and the door. Sometimes he'd wet his lips and watch me in the glass. In a funny way I was feeling sorry for him. Being like he was and Uncle Dudley not that way, he likely wondered what the hell was next. And now Uncle Dudley was talking to Red about Mexico. Sometimes I even wondered about Uncle Dudley myself. But you couldn't wonder long about any one thing because in no time another wonder was there. After while you just gave it up. But take a man like Mr. Liszt who taught music and talked about souls —for a man like that it must be hell to think about him. You can think of some people and make one soul do. But I never heard of a soul that Uncle Dudley would fit. He did most the things good souls should do but dam near all of them they shouldn't. There was two kids I knew just half Navajo because of him. The boy looked like Uncle Dudley would if his own Dad had been Uncle Dudley. That was one better than Uncle Dudley was himself. He was like the idea of Uncle Dudley really worked out. And he was half Indian and could sit and look at you.

Everybody awake was busy looking at maps. Uncle Dudley was explaining the reason Chicago looked so far was because there was so much printed in between. It was so bumpy Mr. Liszt couldn't measure it very well. But anyone could see we were only a third of the way and at that rate it really would be spring in Chi. And still we were making better time than coming out. Going west we'd been two weeks from Santa Fe to L.A.—and here we were all ready east to Santa Fe. I pointed that out and Uncle Dudley felt pretty good. It was Billy the Kid country through here and Uncle Dudley was telling about him—and reciting a poem about a highwayman. It had a part about the landlord's red-lipped daughter that he did pretty well. It made you wonder why there weren't a lot more highwaymen. I tried to think of Uncle Dudley on a horse and with the moon behind him— but like he said the horse dropped out of it. He wasn't a landlord either but he'd sure have done all right by the girl. Once he got to the place and got off the horse, he would have been O.K. I think he'd even been better—I think he'd even got away with her.

Now he was talking about the Land. He never said country when what he meant was Land. Country was what somebody owned and had a sign on—the Land was the whole dam works. And being where we were he was talking about Carlsbad. There was a cave down there like a hollow mountain and with valleys inside. And there was a stalagmite, which is one that drips up, sixty million years old. It was the most important little thing in America, he said. It was like being born —you had to get that far to get anywhere. It was like a piece of Time you could touch, walk around, and see. It was like the first idea Time ever had. Standing down there, he said, was as near to being something as he could stand it—if he got any closer he'd drop dead on the spot. The place was like a landing, he said, between Heaven and Hell. He'd never been so low and yet never felt so high. And you were never quite the same guy when you came out. Like the time I was picked to be the person to be sawed in half.

And now he was talking about a cold night we'd had. That meant that he wanted them to feel that it wasn't cold now. It was just out of Flagstaff and we'd spent all night in the car. When we got to Flagstaff I couldn't feel, I didn't know whether I was steering or not, and the fellow in the Chinese restaurant soaked my hands in a pan of ice. All the time he fed me with chop sticks, then he gave me a pair.

I had them till they broke the night I slept in West-lake Park. That's as nice a park to sleep in as I've ever come across. The cops chase the people out at twelve so you can really sleep. And in the morning there are swans in the lake and more dam birds than you've ever seen, and a place where you can brush your teeth and wipe off with paper towels.

When we stopped for coffee I could see we were in for a night. It was one of those Panhandle winds that never inhale at all. The man had some egg crates in the rear and we boarded up the north side of the car, running strips of paper and cardboard in and out. That helped plenty but besides the wind it was really cold. We had to stop for coffee in Clovis again.

Out of Clovis Red got up front and Uncle Dudley folded up the spares, he and Olie getting down on the floor. We had one more flat near Hereford which I got through because it was Hereford—and because I wanted to stand and look at the sky. Just ten miles away I'd looked at it eight or nine hours a night. I'd learned the *Ode to the West Wind* there and some of Shakespeare's sonnets and a lot of Browning that sounded good but didn't make sense. I'd had a lantern on the seat and would read going against the wind, then recite it with the wind stiff on my back. That way I could hear it above the tractor roar. The *West Wind* was my favorite but I really thought it was pretty silly since it was plain he didn't know any-thing about a Wind. What he had in mind was like an electric fan. When you come in from a night and cross the yard like a catboat tacking, and sleep with your mouth full of sand and don't know it—then you know a wind. Or when you wake up at night like dreaming and feel a weight on the house like water and while you're looking the window just pops like a bag. And then one night you jump up like you're scared and feel the sky is on its way down, and the sound in your ears is like the whisper ahead of a storm. And then you learn—after while—that that means the wind is gone. And it takes you days to get used to the sound of quiet again.

But just knowing that gave me a new slant on what I read. I could see that what a man talked about was hardly ever the thing he named. Like Uncle Dudley talking about Time talked about himself. Instead of Wind I could put something else and it usually sounded just as good—and if you knew something about wind it made better sense. That made it tough for people without much on the ball. But it made it pretty soft for Uncle Dudley and people who had. Uncle Dudley didn't know some things from Adam but he could talk about them just like he did and maybe tell you more about them than a guy who knew all the words. For when you come right down to it the last word is just a name too. And if you can't throw your own light on it it's still in the dark. And Uncle Dudley was the real McCoy, not a gadget that threw your own light back—like the signs on the road that are off till your own lights are on.

When we got under way Uncle Dudley was fishing around in his coat. I knew what he wanted now that he was down on the floor. When we were flush he'd bought a harmonica with a gadget for sharps and flats—he didn't know how to use it but he liked the idea O.K. He liked anything that had something he could fiddle with. On a plain harmonica he wasn't bad—you could tell what he was playing half the time—but on this one it was just no go. It was all so fancy you couldn't tell what it was. Besides that he liked to waw-waw too much and use his hands. Trouble was he was good enough to pick you up before he'd let you down—making you wonder half the time if it was you, or if it was him. Then he always played too long and got his mouth sore. So when you'd really like to hear him he had a sore mouth and couldn't play—till you'd forgotten about it and didn't want it—then it was there. But on a night like this anything helped. Mr. Liszt felt so good about it he could hardly sit still, but when he made a noise it was always some other song. Red and me knew how lousy it was but we didn't mind.

About three o'clock we were in Amarillo, driving slow through the smell of oil and the lights blinking on the derricks back from the road. People were sitting in cafés and having a hell of a time. I couldn't help thinking of Natchez and how he would have liked it here. We all piled out and had a good meal of ham and eggs. Even Mr. Demetrios and Pop came in. There was a machine in the corner that played a violin like the one in Hastings when I was a kid. It was in a glass case and when you dropped in a nickel it played. The one in Hastings was during the war and in a Japanese restaurant with lights on the walls. We always brought our own sugar and ate black bread. It was very special with dim lights at night and a man who did nothing but pour water. Pour water and laugh at anything my Uncle Harry said. Uncle Harry always left a quarter under his plate. That made me sick because I knew a man who would sell six Hershey bars for a quarter—and then give me two cents for the tinfoil besides. It used to make me so sick I didn't like to go. But the violin and the twenty-mile ride were worth it after all.

By the time we came outside it was getting light. But here we were already in Texas, and Oklahoma not far away, where I would have to remember about the dips. Instead of telling you to go slow they just put dips. We were six days in Tulsa once just after one dip. Uncle Dudley started—but his mouth was sore so he put it away.

We stopped for gas under a sign that said DANCE. He was a tall friendly man with two kids and he was busy cleaning up, the little kids running around helping him. They each had colds and a candy bar and a bottle of orange pop. He'd sweep the floor dirt to a pile and they'd put down their candy and scoop it up, running to the stove and dropping it inside. Then they'd stand sucking their fingers and watch it burn. All of it burned, they'd eat candy again. Big roaches were running around and the little boy would sneak up and step on them, the little girl making a face at the frying sound. Their mother came out and wiped their faces with a wet rag. She was a thin, hungry-looking woman with a face like a man. I drank some coffee but decided I wouldn't eat. I came out and sat in the car and the little girl stood in the door and looked at me. Her hair was cut so she would look like Clara Bow. She got a little sick and let the candy drop but went right on drinking the pop. She liked to fizz it up like Olie and then let it squirt down. Right when the last fizz was gone she leaned over and threw up. It made tears come to her eyes but she didn't bawl, didn't do anything—she just stood and looked at the spot she'd made on the ground. Her mother came and wiped off her front like she'd done it a lot before, then she tipped her head and wiped her mouth out too. They looked at each other and then the mother walked away. The little girl looked back at me but like she was drunk and couldn't quite see good, her eyes really looking at something right in between. Her father came out and she followed him to the car. She watched him putting in gas and then the smell made her sick again;

she bent her head and did it on a puddle of ice. Her Dad came and picked her up and wiped her face again with his hanky, then he hugged her tight and kissed her on both eyes. We drove off and when I looked back he waved her hand.

It got so cold we had to stop every hour or so. In Oklahoma City even Mr. Demetrios came in. Standing around the stove he began to smell and the restaurant man kept looking at the wood; it was the same kind of smell wood has when a dog's been around. We were so busy watching him smell we didn't notice it had started to snow, and when I looked out the top of the car was white. But that was something we couldn't help while the clutch was something we'd have to—slipping so bad on even the little grades I had to run for them all. Once I'd fixed the clutch on the Studie with a can of Dutch Cleanser —but this was worse. By just keeping my foot on the brake we wouldn't move at all. A man came in with a paper and a picture of the blizzard that was in Chicago, sweeping south he said, and looked at us—then he looked outside. He turned up the collar on his coat and stood in the door. Uncle Dudley called the Auto Club and they said this was nothing, this was nothing at all, we ought to be in Little Rock now they said. Uncle Dudley said no—he had relatives there. The fellow didn't say any more and Uncle Dudley hung up.

He bought a White Owl and borrowed Mr. Liszt's

coat and went back downtown toward the tracks. Before we'd got around to talking about him he was back again. He had three second-hand lanterns and a small can of kerosene. One time we'd lived in the Studie a week that way. You don't get hot but then again you don't quite freeze. You sit on the floor with your head out and a blanket spread over your knees; the lantern can breathe and the air beneath is warm. We sat around the stove and trimmed the wicks and filled the lanterns. One of them smelled pretty bad but it had its point. That way Mr. Demetrios didn't smell at all. The restaurant man even stopped smelling the wood. But he was a little peeved so we all had coffee to make him feel better and Uncle Dudley bought two more White Owls. Then we came outside and piled in. Olie and Uncle Dudley sat on the floor and stretched an overcoat over the top—they spread it to take in Pop and Mr. Demetrios' leg. They didn't like it but they didn't say no. We used Mr. Liszt's coat in front and it was new with a nice silk lining, and he didn't like it either but he didn't say no. When you're as cold as that you don't say anything.

Then when I put the car in gear it wouldn't move. The grease had got so stiff it was like the brakes were on and the clutch smoked a little but nothing moved. I took up the floor boards and looked at her. There was a screw for adjustment but it was up as far as it would go—and Dutch Cleanser would never take up the slack this one had. I found a flannel shirt under the seat and tore off the sleeves and the buttons, and then I had Red push in the clutch while I worked it around. The two sleeves fit it about right. I was so cold I hoped it wouldn't work after all—but when I tried it it worked like it was new. I went once around the block to see if I could shift and the restaurant man waved as we went by. The man with the paper just looked and shook his head.

It cleared a little like it was even too cold to snow and the road cracked like thin ice under the car. The wind died but there was no sun. The land stopped like a curtain was hung behind, the houses near but the privies looking far and gray. The little towns were stiff-looking and raw. Maybe a Ford noisy and steaming or a man chopping wood—maybe one store with smoke rising, a light somewhere. Sometimes a woman went between houses, her arms crossed and sucked in tight, bent like an old man and running a stiff little run. Nearly always a man's coat, too big, a shawl on her head. Sometimes I'd honk and sometimes they'd side-look at me. Sideways like a dog moves up an alley, curious what you'd throw. It got dark and we wanted to eat, but nobody talked about stopping, nobody wanted to think of starting up again. Mr. Demetrios chewed at salami without any smell. The piece was too small to hang out again and he just kept it in his hand—he didn't offer any to Pop. Pop didn't move. You couldn't tell by looking at him just what the temperature was—all you could tell was that it was too cold or too hot. He didn't flinch, just sat stiff with his hands in his lap. Then for nearly forty miles there were not even lights anywhere; in an hour we passed only one car on the road. I decided that when I saw lights again I'd stop anyhow. I was thinking of what I'd eat, and how taking my time I would eat it—when I saw them on the left, a far twinkle of them. I speeded up for the drift on the turn but as the lights went around the corner I saw the corner went the other way. I turned, but it was like turning a boat against the wind. We drifted up like on a grass beach and settled there. The twinkle of lights crawled south and whistled not far away. When I stepped outside I dropped in above my knees.

We put one lantern back in the road and piled in the rear. For the first time since corn silk I smoked a cigarette and Red tried to teach me to roll my own. But we couldn't afford to waste tobacco now. So I just watched him and practiced licking one. Mr. Liszt was talking about his home. He'd been a little boy in Salzburg which was a fairy land of snow—but his mother wouldn't let him ski. She was afraid he'd hurt his hands. He took them out from under the blanket and we looked at them. They were like a woman's except for the fine black hair. They looked good, Mr. Liszt said, they always looked good. Then he looked up at us and blinked his eyes. And that was very sad, he said—for they were not. "For I haf no genius," he said, "I haf not a tam bit."

Uncle Dudley looked at him and they both blinked their eyes. Mr. Liszt put his hands away and coughed. "Me neither," said Uncle Dudley, "—once thought I could paint." He pulled out his own hands and spread the palms. They were especially funny being Uncle Dudley's hands. The fingers were long and the thumbs nearly like the fingers—they went with his nose some but none of the rest. "Couldn't paint anything one day that the next day wouldn't make me sick. Instead of catching up I kept laggin behind. I learned to know the real thing about the same time I learned I didn't have it. Hurt some—but my painting hurt worse."

"Your hands like a goddam monkey," said Red. Uncle Dudley wiggled them and grinned. He brought the thumbs over till the little fingers touched.

"Never could climb a tree either," he said.

Red looked around—then brought out his. They were freckled and wiry, the cigarette fingers like iodine. His left hand had a red stone ring that left a green circle around the finger. "Never did a dam thing—but love a woman an slap down a man," he said.

"That's quite a bit this day and age," Uncle Dudley said. Red nodded that he thought so too. We all turned and looked at Olie—Olie just stared. He tried to look like he was thinking—but it didn't work.

"You make fun—" he said.

"Not what it would be," said Uncle Dudley. "Anyone who'd laugh at those hams of yours is just a dam fool, not makin fun." Olie wasn't sure, he stared at the lantern awhile. Then he made up his mind and brought out one. It was just as well for there wasn't room for two in the light. They were hams—but so smooth and clean they were like babies, the skin of the palms pink and soft, hardly any lines. The light blond hair on the back and the fingers was baby's hair.

"My wife—" he said, "she like them." And then he got red. We all laughed and Uncle Dudley patted his back. Olie roared like he was Paul Bunyan, slapping his big knees, and nobody heard the car come up behind. Mr. Demetrios finally noticed the man looking in. He looked like he'd been there quite awhile and was there now because he couldn't move. In the quiet we could hear him swallow, wet his lips.

"How ya, pardner," said Uncle Dudley. "Come right in and show your hand," and Uncle Dudley waved and grinned at him. The man stood nodding his head. "You waiting to pull us out?" Uncle Dudley said. The fellow nodded, swallowed again. I climbed out of the car and followed him back to the road. He got in his truck and fooled around somewhere for a rope. After while he found it and turned and looked at me.

"You live around here?" he said.

"No," I said.

He felt better. Walking back he began to whistle a bit.

We followed the truck into the next town. The truck driver knew a man and he woke him up and they made some coffee, all of us sitting around a little oil stove. He had a bottle but there was only one drink around. But it was enough for Mr. Liszt and he began singing German songs, his eyes very wet and shiny in the lamp. He had a nice voice and nobody said anything. But after one he started to cry and Red began *Frankie and Johnnie,* trying to make everything all right again. But Mr. Liszt could cry louder than Red could sing. He knew somebody called Magdalene and he kept calling her name—somebody who lived upstairs began to beat on the floor. There was nothing to do but load him in the car. For a mile or so he went on but it was even too cold for her—he lay back with his head on Red and went to sleep. Then it was all right for an hour or so. But after an hour the coffee began to wear off. I remember coming into a town named HOPE and counting the lights on the street corners—but I don't remember leaving the town at all. And here we were at least a half mile the other side, which is pretty good driving when your eyes are closed. And I'd even picked a ditch that was drift level with the road, and except for an elevator feeling there'd been no feeling at all. Everybody else was still asleep. The engine was still running and the wheels whining in the snow; when I shut off the engine the quiet woke them up. The lights spread a fence on the snow and back in the field was a kind of barn, the doors open so you could see right through. There was no wind at all and so quiet it didn't seem real. I even took off my glove to see if my hand would get cold. It did, so I put it back on again.

"What's up?" said Red.

"Well—" I said, and felt Uncle Dudley's hand on my back.

"We in again, Kid?" he said. I just turned on the brights so they could see. It brought the barn up close and we could look in. There was no house around, just the barn sagging there. The walls buckled just a little like Pop's pants at the knees.

"That a tin barn?" said Uncle Dudley.

"Yeah," I said. Uncle Dudley sat up.

"Pretty nice here," he said. "But if that's a tin barn—and a little wood—"

He got out of the car and waded into the lights. He caught the seat of his knickers on the fence and I had to turn on the bright ones again—then he walked in the barn, and after a moment he came back and waved. I got out because I had things to do and Red and Olie helped Mr. Liszt—he was still saying Magdalene but not like he meant it much. Mr. Demetrios and Pop got down on the floor. I took one lantern and we turned off the lights, followed Uncle

Dudley's tracks to the barn. He was inside piling corn stalks up for a fire. There was no floor and right where we stood there was no roof on the thing—a big square hole open on the sky. One of the cribs had part of a floor, enough wood for a really good fire, and a two-cow manger was ankle deep with cow pies. "Everything here but a bolt hole to stare at—a bolt hole and a fender to park your feet." Uncle Dudley looked around like he might see one. We pulled up some floor boards to pile on the fire and underneath were some sweet corn cobs, so dry they burned like paper, a clean bright flame. We let it burn real hot a spell until the tin walls threw the heat back, then we banked it a little with cow pies and sat around. It was soon too warm and comfy for talking; we just soaked up the fire. Uncle Dudley spread out on some cobs and no sooner stopped squirming than he was asleep. I used his leg to roll him over and he didn't mind. Olie got some cobs and did the same thing. Red and Mr. Liszt slept like they were, leaning on each other and the tin wall, the tin so warm it felt hot to your hand. I built the fire up again and banked it with pies. I tried the cobs but I wasn't that sleepy so I thawed a bunch of cow pies—while they were still warm and pretty smelly I stretched out on them. I lay there awhile looking at the hole in the roof. Once I woke up when I heard a car, the motor idling back on the road; then the lights bounded away and I went back to sleep. I didn't wake up again till someone was shaking me. I looked up at Mr. Liszt, his hair all mussed, his eyes like an owl. He looked frozen to death and was standing there without his coat.

"They're gone!" he said. "Efery-tink is gone!" I sat up and Uncle Dudley sat up too. Mr. Liszt wet his lips and waited until I said who? "Both!" he said. "Both of them—baggash too!"

"Baggage?" said Red.

"Efery-pody's!"

Uncle Dudley got up from the cobs. Red and Olie stood up; they looked at me and I got up too. Then we all walked to the door and looked at the car. The can for oil was still on the running board—but nothing else.

8

WE ALL DECIDED it was a pretty nice job. They'd even thought of letting the air out of the tires. Better than that, they'd even thought of taking the pump, then they'd flagged somebody with the lantern and hitched a ride. All in all it was a pretty nice job. When a job is as good as that you don't even mind it so much—we came back to the barn and sat around the fire. Then I walked into town and borrowed a pump.

Nobody said anything about what they'd lost. All I'd lost was pants and a shirt, which I needed since I'd slept on the cow pies—but otherwise I was glad to see them gone. The pants were two years old and I'd grown some. Mr. Liszt was hard put for a coat since he couldn't pump and keep warm, so we made him go back and stand by the fire. What money anybody had must have been in their pants. Now and then Red would remember something and stand up straight and swear like hell—then he'd feel better and start to pump again. When we were ready the fellow who owned the pump pulled us out.

Then the car was so light it bounced all over the road and I had to stop and let out some of the air. The rear end seemed like an empty boxcar. Uncle Dudley and Olie still sat on the floor. When we felt we'd got somewhere and were hungry again instead of peeved, we stopped and had a round of ham and eggs. The man set the coffee pot on the table and let us pour. And then it was funny how we began to feel. I could see all of them but Mr. Liszt felt like me. Like when I was a kid and off on a hike somewhere. You start out with a nifty pack and all the gadgets for everything, then one by one you let them drop, your hands are free. Then at last you begin to feel like you're getting somewhere. Maybe like a man feels to lose his woman, his home and his job—I wouldn't know but I've heard them talk that way. For the first time you sort of feel like you're breathing free. And I know that feeling when I feel it—and they had it now. Except Mr. Liszt, or people who weren't built that way. People who felt lost without things like Uncle Dudley felt when he had them. Like I felt the time I got the suit with the two pair of pants.

There was a barbershop next door and they all had a shave. I looked in the mirror on the gum machine but the fuzz on my lip was still the same—I combed my hair and tried a center part. I was beginning to see I had a funny face. It was just like Uncle Dudley had said, it had to make a compromise, seeing as how my Mother was swell and my Dad like Uncle

Dudley. It was a face, Uncle Dudley said, that had to make up its mind. If my Dad's mind decided on my Mother's face I'd have something, he said. And since it did once there was some chance it would do it again. But he said not to worry as that was one thing a woman decides.

I walked up and down to keep warm until they came out. It was a clear cold day but getting warmer, the storm had passed. There was a cat lying in a window where the morning sun came in, the tip of her tail just twitching, her eyes closed. She looked so dam comfy she made you mad. Uncle Dudley said cats had it all over dogs, dogs being like too many women, liked for the way they like you, not what they are. And the less they were anything themselves the better they were liked. All the stuff about man's greatest friend was so much crap. It showed how far a man would go to get someone to lick his hand and never have any doubts as to what a swell guy he was. You couldn't sell a cat such a bill of fare. She had her own what, and you had to meet her halfway. It wasn't for nothing, Uncle Dudley said, some women were called cats. But it was a dog-brained goof who thought he knew the reason why. A good woman has her own what and like a good cat won't sell herself short—she'll take just so much molly-coddling then she draws the line. It takes more than fresh hamburger and a scratching to get at her soul. And when she goes a-wooing you and everyone else can go to hell. They'll howl and scratch some because they really know what it's all about. And there's something to show for it the next time you come around.

Red and Olie were standing in front looking around. There was a line on Red's neck where the shaving soap had stopped and before the hairs on his chest began. His face was shiny like an apple skin. Olie's face was pink and soft-looking like his hands. They were both just standing there like men do when they've done something—different than if they'd just come out and stood there. Like you stand when you come out after a meal. You're between things somehow and you're more like part of the corner; you haven't made up your mind just what is coming next. When a man like that looks you over you don't mind. You know it's because it's the only thing right then to do. And when I walked up they looked me over, not really seeing me at all, just looking at me because I happened to be there.

"Well, Kid," said Red. "Where the hell we off to now?" I acted like I was considering where. Red took out his pack of Camels and made a jerk with his wrist that brought one up where he could lip it free. I liked the way he could do that. There was something expert about it, like watching Natchez chalk his cue. If I ever smoked I was going to do it that way. Red offered me one and I shook my head. I wanted him to see the difference between my smoking last night and not smoking now—and he saw it and didn't kid me about it at all. I looked through the window at Mr. Liszt still in the chair. His face looked small with his glasses off and his Adam's apple big. Uncle Dudley was sitting talking to someone. He was looking again like I liked to see him, like a fellow you can't quite figure out, which was sure enough Uncle Dudley to a tee. The other man was a character but he was just one character—the thing about Uncle Dudley was that he was the works. He looked a little bit like all the characters you ever saw. But the part that was Uncle Dudley was the something more. That's why you couldn't see him at first look, why it took so much time.

"My wife race hell—" Olie said, just out of nowhere. He was just catching up with what happened last night. But you could see just thinking of his wife made him feel good. He opened his coat and felt around to hook his thumbs. He'd stopped wearing the hat and that way he didn't look so bad—not since the suit had stopped being the kind of suit it was. Now it was just something funny that he was half wrapped in.

Uncle Dudley came out and played around at looking over the car. I knew he'd heard something pretty good because he never did that unless he had—doing that instead of cuffing someone around. He chewed a good thing over that way, getting all the juice. Then maybe if he thought you'd get it he'd tell you—if he didn't he'd say let's go. "Let's go—" he said, and climbed in the rear. Then he noticed Mr. Liszt was still covered with soap, some of it in his hair. So he thought of it again and just sat gloating over it.

Near Texarkana the ground was clean, it hadn't snowed at all. We drove around the streets awhile like we were looking for them, Uncle Dudley half afraid they might be there. Mr. Liszt asked a policeman and gave him his name. There was one man in town who bought second-hand clothes but we didn't recognize anything. Red bought himself another sailor hat. It was a little too small and looked like a kind of pot but nobody said anything.

Over in Arkansas Mr. Liszt began to sneeze. We stopped while Uncle Dudley fixed him, filling him up with hot lemonade, soda, and quinine pills. He kept sneezing so we stretched him out in the rear. Olie came up front and Uncle Dudley held Mr. Liszt's head in his lap, telling him how he had some German and how far back. We had relatives in Little Rock so we didn't go there. We went straight east through El Dorado where we had two flats right in town—one coming in and the same dam tire going out. I had to buy a new tube and Uncle Dudley gave me five dollars. When I came back with the change he said, "You keep it, Kid." That's what he always said when it was the last. I put the three-forty in my pocket and fixed the tire.

What made me feel funny was that I didn't feel

much at all. Here we had three-forty between us and Chicago and I didn't seem to mind. I was getting so dam much like Uncle Dudley I was a shame. We went on and in the next town I spent two-eighty for gas. That left sixty cents plus a dime I had. It was Saturday and the little towns were crowded with old jalopies and thin-looking men in faded blue jeans. A man with anything else on looked out of place. They were good lean-looking men but bent like ditch grass at the top. They had good-looking faces but they'd all worked too hard. The women didn't look much like them at all, they just looked like hell. Once they'd stopped being girls and were women they looked the same. Some of them looked like they'd stopped being girls pretty young. The Negroes looked poorer but you wouldn't say that was how they were. But you'd say being poor was one thing they all were. It was a bigger part of them than what color they were and they could stand and talk and not see color there. That was different than a black and white man up north. Up north the biggest part they had was pretty small. A black man was a nigger here and maybe a colored man up there—but all of that was what you called him, not what he was. He was like anybody else and he'd like to talk with you. Being poor together is really something you can talk about.

Uncle Dudley was saying what the difference was. The north went in for bundling and the south for basterds, he said. The difference was how much you liked the real thing. Maybe the south liked to rub it in and the north liked to rub it out—each making the other one look a little worse. But whatever a man had a nose for he could get a full smell of down here. All the crap in a man's system and most of the good.

We stopped twice more to refill Mr. Liszt, once to let it out. We had coffee once and coffee was all we had. I began to remember a little bit what hungry was. The first two days are pretty hard—then it isn't so bad. Then before it gets worse Uncle Dudley has something. You get so you don't really worry when he is along. In this case he'd ask Red or Olie like he did before. If that didn't work we'd have to pick up passengers again. If that didn't work we'd have to sell the car again. If that didn't work we'd have to ride the freights again. And that always worked so we didn't worry much. Because in Chicago there was Monkey Wards buying kids for thirty cents an hour or the Y where I could talk about Life and lead the prayers. And in a week Uncle Dudley would be right in the groove. Soon as I could pay for the storage and he could get his clothes. And the box of cards saying just T. Dudley Osborn—till he made up his mind.

About dark I could tell by the fields the river was near. We'd have to ferry to Greenville and to do that we'd need a dollar, and Uncle Dudley would have to ask them then. There were pines and cabins now, the smoke rising without a wrinkle, making me think of the Log Cabin syrup can. The yards in front of the shacks were smooth and the pickaninnies hung on the fences or stood where you couldn't see them in the door. Just their eyes and whatever scrap of rag they had. The windows were just board shutters drawn closed. We made a quick turn beside a lake that once must have been part of the river and then the road entered a small town. I had just time to see a brick courthouse and a man standing there. Then all hell broke loose and dragged at the rear. My foot went to the floor on the brake, but we didn't stop, nothing happened—just more hell than ever hanging on behind. Doors opened and people ran out and stared. We came to the tracks and just like in Kansas City, whatever it was caught there, we couldn't go on. There was a sick, gritty crunch—then that was all. The people just stayed where they were; the road was clear. Uncle Dudley got out and crossed the street, bought a cigar.

It had finally happened just like Zeke had said. Snapped off in front of the housing and then dropped to drag in the street—until the tracks where it had twisted for a right turn. The front had then gone on a little ways. There was a train in an hour or so and it took three mules that long to move her—Uncle Dudley having the time of his life. He'd always wanted a team of mules and the Negro let him work them—Uncle Dudley hollering Gee—then Whizz when he meant Haw. He got the mules so futzied up they wouldn't do anything. It took everything the Negro had to get them organized again and the car off before the train was due. The point being it was coming through—not just in.

We built a fire down near the water and sat around. Mr. Liszt was blowing instead of sneezing and his nose was red. But Uncle Dudley looked him over and said it was good. Nobody said anything about the car. There wasn't anything to say and it made things kind of nice, falling apart right where she did. I could see Uncle Dudley thought it was pretty swell. He bought a bag of potatoes and a quarter pound of butter, and a can of grapefruit pieces for Mr. Liszt. We baked the potatoes down in the coals. When it was dark we noticed the people back on the street. They were all Negroes and just their eyes showed. The garage man had said the town had about eight hundred people and during the winter four of them were white. None of the four was around there yet. Now and then a Negro woman would laugh like nobody else knows how to laugh, and was like one woman laughing for everyone. Olie didn't seem to notice and Red just looked at Uncle Dudley—Uncle Dudley was looking his best in a long time. He was sitting there licking his fingers and humming a tune. Then right in the middle he stopped humming—looked up at them. He wiped his hands on his knicker socks and stood up. We watched him walk up the bank and through the center, all of them turning away and watching him. They just stood with their backs to us, not turning again. After a little while they began to walk away—off where they'd been looking, like to a fire. Soon there was no one on the bank at all. We could see the tops of the street lights, the glow over the town. I began to wonder and at about the same time so did Red. Olie and Mr. Liszt were half asleep on a log. We got up and walked to where we could peek down the street—it looked like half the town was huddled around the car. Uncle Dudley was standing on the hood with the lantern hooked in his arm and his right hand up like he'd been lecturing. Only he was through talking—just standing there. He looked like a Paul Revere statue of some kind. Then we could hear other voices and when they called they raised their hands, the big palms like milk chocolate in the light. Then no more hands, no talk at all. Uncle Dudley waved the lantern like a brakeman, sat it down, clapped his hands. He slid off the hood and walked back in the crowd. We could see where he was like you see a dog in tall grain, the heads bending a little, turning aside. It stopped near the center, then it came our way. Uncle Dudley came out on the street under the lamp. He was still carrying the lantern and about halfway he stopped to light his cigar, raising the glass chimney to get at the flame. At the

148

edge of the bank he stood and looked at us. "Twenty-seven bucks," he said. "Not bad—considering."

"No," said Red.

"No—" I said, "not bad."

Then he left us there and went off with the lantern to look for wood.

9

I WAITED till there was light enough to see. They were still asleep and fuzzy with dew like the grass. The lake was quiet as a pond of new ice, not a scratch anywhere. Just a rim of white suds like Mr. O'Toole's hair. Somewhere in the town a wagon was moving, the wheels in the dust. Then it crossed a piece of pavement and I heard the horse. He walked with a slow, floppy plod like his head was low. Then they were in the road again and the wheels in the dust.

I got up quiet and walked to the bank. I went down the street to where I could get a good look at her. There was a sign on the front—*This belong Henry Poke*, it said. Even like she was with her rear end dragging she had class. The little wheels did it somehow; they kept her low. A wagon like that never looked like a piece of junk. She might not be able to move but just sitting there she had class—you knew she'd done some dam fine moving in her day. I went up and had one more look under the hood. She was pumping a little oil on two plugs—but not much. It was worth twenty-seven bucks just to lift the hood on her. I took out the front plug, then I let the hood back down. I went around on my side and looked at the dash. We were 2,250 miles out of L.A. I got in and sat there awhile working the clutch. Then I got out and took up the floor. Pushing the clutch in with my hand I tore off a piece of the lining, wrapped it around the plug and put it in my shirt. Then I walked off to where I could see her whole. A rooster crowed, and right away the town was all roosters. I looked back toward the lake and Uncle Dudley was standing there.

"Well—" he said, "you leave anything for Henry?" I didn't say anything. I went down to the water and splashed some of it in my face. When I came back Red was sitting up rubbing his eyes. He offered me a cigarette and I said sure.

We heated some water in a can and boiled some eggs. Uncle Dudley knew how to feel a soft-boiled egg and not spill it—you could eat the whole business right in the shell. It was all part of how he could run a thing. Here was Mr. Liszt with a cold and a woman's kind of hands, sleeping on a beach and sucking an egg through the top. I'd seen it before but it was always good. He did it mostly by just not doing it at all. He never said, now we'll do this—he just did it himself. And since you hung around Uncle Dudley you were doing it too. Maybe like me you'd wonder about it, but you wouldn't change. And pretty soon it just seemed the easiest thing to do. Sleep where you were and eat on the fire you had. There was a restaurant right on the street selling eggs and toast for a dime—and we had a dime, but here we were sitting right here. Waiting for Uncle Dudley to peel another egg.

After breakfast he split the twenty-seven bucks five ways. Mr. Liszt was so happy Uncle Dudley asked him how much money he had. He took out his billfold and he had two dollars some. Red said Hell, he had plenty of dough, and he gave him his five— Olie got red again and tossed in his. That would buy him a bus ticket, Uncle Dudley said. And since he had a cold he'd better use it and get along. Mr. Liszt began to sneeze and his eyes got wet. I began to see why it was he kept thinking of soul. It was just a way of getting more out of a thing than it had. He'd probably think we were all better now than we really were. Just like another time he'd probably think we were worse. He might get over that and be a pretty nice guy with Uncle Dudley around. But here he was leaving and going back to himself again.

We all rode out of town on a wagon levee bound. You could walk faster but it was somehow nice to ride. It was still early but already a little warm. A Negro stood on the porch of his shack shaving himself in a piece of cracked glass, his suspenders hanging down on his light green pants. His white shoes were like bright holes in the porch. It made me remember that it was Sunday—then we heard the bells.

The driver was saying the river was high, looked like a flood. He was a huge black man that made even Olie look small—his back was as broad as the three-seater buckboard seat. He kept talking to the mule then tipping his head to hear what he'd say—then he'd laugh an say, Well, ah declare! It was the mule that told him there would be a flood. Everytime he go near the river he go slower, he said. Come to the point where he soon ain't goin at all. And right then it was goin to flood, all over hell. He kept lapping the mule with the reins like you pet something. There was no hair at all on him there, like an old boot.

A white man came running out of a house and climbed on. His house was just like the others except the chimney was white. A white rocking chair sat in the door. His wife was out in the back hanging out clothes. She wore a sunbonnet and you couldn't see her face—her long skirts made a little dust cloud when she moved. "That's a goddam fine place," said the man, seeing us look at it so hard, "eighty years old and that side wood as good as new."

"Mighty clean lookin place," Uncle Dudley said.

"My name's Hogue," said the man. "A Hogue built it right heelin the war and it's gonna be a Hogue place so long's I'm around. Goddam wood today is turpentined to death. No blood in the stuff—how the hell you expect it to last? Now I'm lookin forward to

153

paintin it up. Can't make up my mind just what color—kinda like that white on there now."

"I think white'd be pretty smart," Uncle Dudley said.

"See it easy comin home that way," said Mr. Hogue. I thought he meant it funny and I started to laugh. Then I saw he didn't—he didn't at all. He filled his mouth with cut plug and turned to slap the big Negro—cuffing him like a little guy always cuffs a really big man. "You big basterd," he said, "how the hell are you?"

"I'm high," said the big guy.

"Why, you big sunuvabitch," he said. "D'you hear that?" He looked at Uncle Dudley then he looked at me. "The way these goddam niggers enjoy themselves makes a man sick—they so goddam dumb they don't know they hard off." Mr. Hogue cuffed him again, grinned at him. "I'm gonna be high too," he said, "I'm gonna be so high my bottom's up—but next time you unload me in the yard see you watch my pants. You big enuf," he said, "to pick a man up by more'n his pants."

"I pick him up where he stick high," the big fellow said. Mr. Hogue shifted his chew. He spit a fat wad back in the road that raised the dust. Then he noticed for the first time how funny we looked. Olie's suit had shrunk all over and the pants wouldn't sit down; they were tight where his thighs got big and hung like a pipe. Red had rolled his navy pants high.

154

Mr. Liszt had got over being happy and looked something like the pants to his suit. They were good pants for what they'd been through—but that was too much. I hadn't seen before that he had a celluloid collar, for they're clean where they should be dirty, dirty where they'd be clean. The top edge was shiny like the rim of a cup. His little bow tie was unhooked and bent to one side. He still held his hands like a man with some buttons off, but it wasn't so bad any more, you didn't have to look. He still did it but it didn't mean the same thing any more.

Mr. Hogue was trying to read the letters on my sweatshirt. But LAKEVIEW wouldn't mean anything to him or the C for being captain so I just let my coat hang where it did. But it made me think of going to college again. Playing mixed doubles with one of those girls and winning a cup to let her keep it, both of your names on it together somewhere. I was thinking of that and how bad my serve was, when the wagon stopped. I turned around and the smooth-banked levee was there. Two, maybe three dozen people stood on the top, all of them black men showing their teeth, some of them all snaked up, some of them just in blue jeans. They called to the big Negro, then went on joking again. We got off and walked up the trail, the ground hard as a shanty yard. On the top there was the river—and she was high. She was higher than I'd ever seen her before. High and dirty and out mid-stream you could see her roll, see her sucking in the slow water from the sides. Up a quarter mile the ferry was drifting in. Clear across, where the boats looked tiny, even the big sidewheelers anchored there —was a concrete levee higher than the trees. Tom Sawyer had something to do with something there. I'd played Tom Sawyer in Omaha in the eighth grade graduation play and a kid named Mulligan had played Huck Finn. I hadn't known till then just what was wrong with him. For there was something wrong with the way he stood around, which was bad since all he did was stand around. I don't know how it looked from the seats but it sure looked wrong to me, because he was wearing old clothes but he looked like he had his new suit on. The thing was, he always looked like he had his new suit on. When his part was over he'd hurry out in the toilet to dress and then come in to show what really nice clothes he had. Outside of that he was a pretty good kid. Only some of that was in everything he did. He didn't like to play games at night because no one could see him—which was all to the good but he didn't see it that way. He called me Pal and I called him Pal but something was wrong. Last time I saw him I'd been to New York and he'd been to Council Bluffs, which you could see from the room where he was born. Yet he never got around to asking where I'd been, letting his ice cream melt while he told me about Council Bluffs.

When I got off the ferry I had $5.25. That's a lot of money when you stop gassing a car. I've gone from

Omaha to Salt Lake for a buck and a half. I would have gone farther but they switched the cars around and when I got out of the hatch it was Cheyenne.

We walked Mr. Liszt to his bus and Uncle Dudley fixed his tie—we all shook hands and wrote his friend's address down. We all did it and we all knew it was no use. We stood outside and talked because Olie couldn't sit down and when the bus pulled out we stood and waved. Then we walked along behind it past the stores.

We walked north along the tracks toward the edge of town. The New Orleans express went by and smoothed the grass flat on the levee; little specks of coal dust went along the road. Old houses sat away back and the yards were dark with trees, very quiet like a funeral was around. The sidewalk was noisy so we walked along in the grass. There was a low haze on the river, thinning clear. We moved over single file to let a truck pass. Another car passed but pulled over and stopped off the road. It was a sedan with a lot of room in the back. The fellow in front was grinning and had a kind of chauffeur's hat—he looked back through the rear window and waved his hand. "Bygod," said Red, "I really like it down here. Down here they stop and flag at you—bygod that's nice." We came along side and the other man up front got out. He was fat and still laughing at something the other fellow had said, and the barrels of the gun resting on his belly bounced up and down. He held it crooked in his arm like something that was always there. He didn't say anything, just opened the door and went on laughing, wiggled his thumb for us to get inside. Uncle Dudley stopped and looked at the gun and then at his face. It was pink and hairless looking with very small eyes. They looked at you once, then if you were looking they looked away. Uncle Dudley got in without saying a word. We all got in and the fellow closed the door. There was a glass plate between the front and the rear and they went on laughing, not saying anything. The other one turned the car around and we went back into town.

Two Men on a Horse

I

I SAT in a room with a skylight in the roof. There was a chair and a pair of scales with a rod to measure your height and a picture of Woodrow Wilson on the wall. I weighed myself and toward evening I weighed less. There was some writing on the door like you find on a backhouse wall, only better than the kind you find in the north. That is, it was worse so it was better for what it was for. Sometimes I could hear men laugh like they were trying pretty hard and once I heard Uncle Dudley really laugh. Once I heard Olie laugh like Paul Bunyan would. I took the five-dollar bill I had and put it where Uncle Dudley had showed me the time we were in jail in Trinidad. I left the twenty-five cents and my scout knife in my pants. There was a light in the ceiling but no place to turn it on, the glass full of dead flies and gum wrappers. I sat on the scales and then I sat on the floor. When it's getting dark there is something about sitting on the floor. Lights came on in the town and made the clouds look low and pigeons came and walked up and down on the roof. Then they left and bats came so near I could hear them fly.

The door opened before the light went on. I had been asleep and one man was already inside, opening camp chairs and leaning them on the wall. Three other cops came in and sat down. They had just finished eating and they picked their teeth and looked at me; the fat one with the pink face winked and grinned. He had a grin that looked friendly until I grinned at him and then it was like I'd caught him peeking somewhere. Like he'd just turned from a keyhole somewhere. I kept looking at him and he turned and spit on the floor.

"Whose turn?" one of them said.

"McCord—" said the fat one. "McCord's turn now."

"Crap," said McCord, and they all looked at him. He was a little man in a worn blue uniform. All the edges were worn through like most streetcar conductors and he looked like one that had a very bad breath. But his badge was bright and there was polish in the cracks in between. "Crap," he said, and rubbed his heel where he spit on the floor. He looked across at the big man who had brought in the chairs and the big one looked away. He was the man who had driven the car and brought us in. He kept his hat pushed back like he wasn't really wearing it at all. "Biscuit—" said McCord. "You're takin the kid."

"Yeah-yeah," said the last one. "You take him, Biscuit." He was as small as McCord but older and he had a paunch. He was narrow and thin at the top and his face was thin except at the throat, a piece of skin like a turkey gobbler hanging there. It flapped up and down like a gobbler when he talked.

"O.K., Chief," Biscuit said, and looked at the Chief and then at McCord. McCord spit on the floor and stepped on it again. Biscuit came over and stood looking at me. He took a piece of gum from his pocket and unwrapped it. "Where you from, Kid?" he said.

"Jesuscrist," said McCord, "think he don't know that?"

"Yeah," said the Chief, "think he doan know that?"

"Use your goddam head," said McCord. "Screw him up—ask him something smart. Ask him where he's goin—ask him why he's goin there." Biscuit threw the gum wrapper at the light and it went in. Some of the flies weren't really dead and started buzzing around.

"That three outa five for you," said the fat one.

"Yeah—" Biscuit said.

"Gee-*zus*-crist!" said McCord. He took off his hat and he hadn't any hair at all. His head was so smooth it looked naked and made you turn away, like he'd taken off more than his hat but hadn't meant to. He put it on quick and looked at Biscuit again.

"Where you goin, Kid?" Biscuit said.

"Chicago," I said. McCord got up and kicked his chair down, left the room. He slammed the door so hard the light rattled and began to swing. Biscuit stood and watched, staring at the flies.

"Jesuscrist," said the Chief, "—think he doan know that—do you now?" He looked at the fat one then at Biscuit again. They didn't pay any attention to him and he looked at me. He unbuttoned the flap on his gun and took it out, pointed it at me. He sighted down the barrel with one eye and then he belched. He looked up like to see if he had hit me— then belched again. "Got him," he said, "got him that time," and put his gun away. He couldn't get the flap fastened again so he left it loose.

"Let him cool," said the fat one. "Let him cool—"

"Now you talkin," said the Chief. "Biscuit, we gonna let him cool. Let him cool awhile an then he talk—won't he now?" Biscuit nodded his head. He came over and reached me his hand, pulled me up. "Oh Jesuscrist," said the Chief. "Let him get up by hisself—" Biscuit looked at me and I got down and then got up by myself. "There—" said the Chief. "O.K. now—Biscuit, you let him cool."

Biscuit took my arm and we walked out in the hall. We went back down to the office where McCord was sitting by the radio listening to a funny program from somewhere. He let us stand till the man stopped talking and the music began. "Well—you frisked him?" he said. Biscuit cuffed the side of my pants. I took out the twenty-five cents and my pocket knife. McCord dropped it in a drawer—then he opened it and looked at the nickels again. He looked at the date of a buffalo nickel I had. He put it in his pocket and put back one of his own. Then he took it out again and held it up to Biscuit's face. "You know what that's worth?" he said.

"Five cents," said Biscuit. McCord tried to laugh. He made all sorts of noises like he was laughing very hard.

"You dumb basterd," he said, "—that's all you know—that's the sense you got. That's worth twenty-two cents. *Twenty-two* cents," he said. He put it back in his pocket and walked to the radio. He went on snickering until the funny man began to talk.

Biscuit took some keys from the wall and led me outside. We crossed the long fenced-in yard to a flight of stairs and a light at the top. There was a light in the room behind and just bars at the door. We walked up the stairs and stood on the landing while he looked for the key.

There was a row of beds along the wall under the light. Along the wall across the room there were toilet booths, the stools gone and beds in two of them. One booth had a door and the bed was clear inside. In the last one there was a stool and a fellow sat with his head in his hands—he was in his underwear and the legs were rolled to the knee. When Biscuit locked the door he looked up, and he was a young fellow, husky, with curly brown hair. He didn't look at me at all but at the bed near the door. A kid maybe ten years old was lying there. He had a thin sharp face and his head went back very fast to a point, the hair growing down and around his face like a roof. He was trying to look at me without opening his eyes.

"Where the hell you been?" said Red, and I turned around. He was lying on a mattress with one end tipped up on the wall. There was a pile of cigarette butts beside him on the floor. "Where the hell you been—you seen Olie?"

"No—" I said.

"They prob'ly let him go. They prob'ly took his wad of dough an let him run. Poor sunuvabitch. He ain't the slightest idea where the hell Detroit is."

"Uncle Dudley here?" I said.

"Back in one of them goddam private rooms. He sure makes me sick—been carryin on like he likes it here. Lyin there smokin his goddam cigar like this was the Biltmore." Uncle Dudley was lying on his back with his toes in the air. There were holes in his socks but he had switched the feet, his toes not showing. He had his little toe where the big hole was but clear inside. "He's prob'ly pooped from laughin," said Red, "—never heard the damned old fool laugh so much. Him and that kid lyin over there just laugh an laugh an laugh. The kid don't know any better but that Uncle of yours is old enough."

"He thinks jails are funny," I said.

"Then he's never been in one. He's been so busy

laughin and enjoyin himself he don't know what it's like." I turned and looked at the kid, still peeking at me. "Don't know what that kid's here for," said Red. "He ain't said a word—all he does is laugh. When he ain't laughin he makes a squeak like a whistle that's meant to be. They call him Peanut after that kind of squeak." When Red said Peanut the kid opened his eyes and stared. He looked something like a rabbit and he could stare the same way without blinking. I looked away at the man on the stool, still just sitting there. With one hand he mussed his hair and watched the dandruff snow. Uncle Dudley made a noise and rolled over on his side.

"You might as well sit right down," said Red, "—an save all the standin around. I swore I wouldn't sit down in all this crap but here I am lyin in it. You might as well lie down right off and enjoy it."

"I've been sittin," I said, "all the time since I seen you." The fellow on the stool got up and backed outside. The seat of his underwear was gone and there was just a hole there, like when a little kid drops the seat of his pants. His behind was firm and spanky and he had good legs. He turned on a faucet high on the wall and watched the water splash in the stool. When it got so high it flushed itself. He stood and scratched his seat, then he walked into the light. He walked right past Red and me and stood in the door.

"All I'd like right now," he said, "—nice plump li'l Hawayan gal."

"Bygod—" said Red, "you're sure as hell easy to please."

"Li'l island—a nice plump li'l Hawayan gal."

"Dewey—" said Red, "you're one of these moonin guys. Here you are in a jail an you're moonin like a calf. There's plenty nice plump little gals but bygod they ain't up here."

"How far's Hawaya?" Dewey said. "How a man go about findin Hawaya?"

"They're all like that," said Red. "They're all crazy as hell up here. And yet that goddam'd Uncle of yours is craziest yet." The kid, Peanut, rolled over on his face. For a while there was nothing, then I heard the squeaky whistle; it was thin and high and seemed to come out of his nose. Dewey turned from the door and looked at him.

"What that kid here for?" said Red.

"Same thing you here for," said Dewey. "Same thing we all here for—somebody got to be here."

"What the hell you mean?"

"Somebody got to be the law," said Dewey. "Somebody got to show we got law in our town."

"This your town?"

"Born and raised," said Dewey.

"Bygod," said Red, "I couldn't help where I was born but I can sure as hell do something about where I'm raised."

"This a nice town," said Dewey. "All in all this a nice town."

"It's a goddam hole—"

"No—" said Dewey, "this a nice town." He walked back to the door and looked out at it. The moon was coming and there were bright spots on the roofs. I could see little scraps of paper in the yard. Peanut went on squealing, a long leak with a whistle at the end. "That goddam kid laugh at anything— he even laugh to see a grown man cry." Peanut rolled over on his face and covered his mouth. He kicked his feet like he was being tickled from behind. "I paddled his little arse till my right hand sore, but it do no good, no good at all." Dewey turned and looked at me. "When you come in?"

"He's with us," said Red. "He's with the old man and me."

"He with that funny old man?" Red nodded his head. Dewey walked away from the door and looked at me. "Yet he look all right—"

"He's O.K.," said Red. "You ain't heard him gigglin, have you?"

"No—" Dewey said, and looked at Peanut again. He stood awhile scratching his seat and whistling *No, No, Nora* very soft. Then he walked to his bed and sat down and looked at his feet. "I'm gettin sick," he said, "workin the roads without fit shoes. I'm gettin to walk like a man with a bad case of clap."

"I won't work 'em bygod," said Red. "I won't move a goddam hand."

"You aroun here awhile an you pay 'em to let you

work. You get tired anything, an first thing you get tired of is sittin aroun."

"Bygod—" said Red.

"You jus save it. You gonna run outa tough too before you know." Dewey lay back and pulled the blanket up to his chin. There was a fellow with black hair beyond him and a fellow with straw-colored hair this side. They all slept with their backs turned to the light. "Besides," Dewey went on, "you likely not really tough. Only really tough man I know lyin over by the crapper now. I been in and out but he been here all the time. He tough—he really tough as hell—but what good it do? Like that funny old man of yourn was sayin—what good it do?"

"What're you in for?" said Red.

"They tell me when I drunk I really tough. But when I ain't drunk I ain't tough at all. Trouble is, soon as I out I seem to get drunk." A car came into the yard and the lights bounced on the wall. Dewey rolled out of bed quick and crossed to the door. He leaned on the bars and looked down the stairs. "Biscuit," he said.

"Yeah?" said Biscuit.

"Got fixins but no paper—see you honey chile get paper?"

"Dewey—" said Biscuit. "you sure as hell be stuntin your growth. If I told your old man you was already smokin he'd beat hell outa you."

"That he would," said Dewey.

"How that new boy?"

"He doin fine."

The door opened and the sound of the radio came up the stairs. Dewey tapped a little dance on his way to bed.

"That Biscuit a good man," he said.

"He's the fat one?"

"That Cupid—Cupid kinda man like to 'vestigate lady crappers all the time. When he was a kid he was always wearin dresses and goin in the ladies side. Now he free to go in when he want to an look aroun."

The man with the yellow hair suddenly sat straight up in bed. He was tall and thin and stared right into the light. Tears came out of his eyes and ran shiny down to his mouth. He looked like he was seeing somebody after a long, long time. Dewey leaned over and pressed him back on the bed. "He dreamin all that," he said. "He really all right—he really O.K. He really one the finest goddam people you ever seen." Now that he was on his back the man cried and shook his head. Dewey pulled the covers up to his chin and patted him. He got quiet like a little boy would, making sounds with his lips. When he stopped and lay quiet we could hear Peanut again. Dewey got in bed and turned his back to the light. " 'Bout time," he said, "that goddam light was goin out." Peanut thought that was pretty funny too. "Didn't I tell you," Dewey said, "that kid laugh at anything. He laugh to see a grown man cry—he laugh at anything you talk." Peanut went on laughing, kicking his feet in the air. They were big feet for a kid—the bottoms flat and broad as a man's. When he stopped kicking I could see the cigar labels around his big toes. One was a White Owl with a piece of fresh gum inside the band. The other one I could just about read when the light went out.

After while I could see the window and under it Red's white hat on his face, like the light was still on, his breathing noisy on the rim. Peanut lay quiet like the switch had turned him off too. I could see the white bottom of the stool and Uncle Dudley's feet, his toes still in the air—there was a moon somewhere and broken glass in the cracks on the stairs. I crossed the floor and buttoning all my buttons got down beside Red. I lay on my back and thought about me being here. If I was brave I wouldn't be here—or I'd be here with a better reason—the one I had only being a reason for getting out. If I was brave I'd be here for a reason for getting in. I would have kicked pink-face in the guts and then taken his gun and paddled his seat and walked him back into town in his shorts. But I wasn't brave, because the first thing I thought of was getting out. I acted like a nice quiet kid because I wanted out. Uncle Dudley had a hand in that for he says it's smart and I still think it is— but it's got nothing to do with whether or not I'm brave. And Uncle Dudley had a hand in that too.

172

Sometimes I wonder, like now, if there's any of me he hasn't a hand in—maybe if I thought about it I'd find there's nothing left. Yet there was somebody there before he came along. I thought I'd seen quite a bit myself before I'd even heard of him and the only reason I went to see him was to see more. He took my Uncle Harry and me to lunch. He was just passing through from a ranch he had somewhere to a farm he had somewhere else. He spent all lunch talking about some little rocks he found around gopher holes all over his ranch. They were like a six-sided pencil and sharpened at both ends. Some were finger thick and some like a kernel of wheat. He said they just came like that, right off the ground. He had a Durham bag full of them and he was just tickled to death that Uncle Harry and me couldn't explain. Uncle Harry brought in God and the names of all sorts of Indians and Uncle Dudley just sat and laughed. He could make a fool out of you no matter what you said. He had a reason for everything but his bag of rocks. And he used all of his reason just to keep your reason away, like people do when you try to get too close to their God. But I didn't see then what I've come to see now. He didn't have it in for God any more than he had it in for reason—the thing was that he wanted his bag of rocks to win. He wanted the Land to know something more than anybody and do something that nobody could figure out. People

173

who want God to win are the same way. But there aren't many of them who can do it with a bag of rocks.

Somebody got up and crossed the floor to the stool. I could hear him scratching his head and swearing quietly to himself, beginning over when he ran out and going back through. Then he turned on the water and let it run a long time. When it was cold he leaned in his head and took a long drink. I could see the white stripe in his shorts and his hands when he wiped them there. Then he went on swearing quietly where he left off.

It was two years before I knew about those rocks. And then I only knew about them and couldn't explain. Best I could do was tell him snowflakes happened the same way. And then I couldn't keep from telling him that snowflakes came down from above.

It made him so mad he sent me a book named "Elmer Gantry" and a magazine called *How to Think* that came every week. I wrote him back that he liked his rocks just like Grandpa liked his God—they both thought they had something you couldn't explain away. I told him he was the same kind of old fool that Grandpa was. I wouldn't have said that if I'd known what an old fool Grandpa really was—but I said it and sent it off airmail. It was winter then and I was working at the Y. It made my Uncle Dudley so

174

peeved he telegraphed offering me a job; he said I was so far gone he couldn't help me by mail. On the other hand he couldn't let me go on like I was. So if I'd take the job he'd see what he could do. Well, I wanted to see Texas so I took the job.

"Hey!" said the fellow who had been swearing, and slapped someone. He slapped him again and the other one turned and said gee-zus-crist. "Who the new boy, Hal?" he said, and cuffed him once more. The one named Hal just lay and scratched somewhere. Then he raised on one arm and looked across at me. His bed was near the other window and he raised his head into the light—it looked very big and shaggy with straw-colored hair. He was a grown man but his face was shy like a little boy. He couldn't see me watching but his eyes blinked and were shy—like they were afraid even their looking might hurt someone.

"He brand new, Kirby," said Hal. "He brand new sometime tonight." Then he fell back like that made him tired and scratched some more.

"He young—" said Kirby. "He look young as hell. An he lyin there like as if he wun't lyin—"

"Sailor boy was doin that too."

"Sailor boy oughta know good bug like up-crawlin better'n down-crawlin—"

"That he should."

"He likely young too—we soon need a nursin

175

mammy up here. They too young to eat egg. Eatin egg an chittlins make 'em sick."

"Cupid the good one to find 'em young. Cupid found little Peanut—Biscuit kinda shamed."

"Helluva lotta good his shamin doin you. Peewee McCord just half his size but let him bark an Biscuit bite. If a man gonna bite I like him to use his own teeth."

"Biscuit like me—he doan wanna bite."

"Bet that new boy ain't thinkin how sweet Biscuit is—"

"You allus thinkin what somebody else thinkin. Bet he ain't thinkin at all—bet he sweet dreamin now."

"Bet he ain't sweet dreamin how sweet you Biscuit is—"

—and then when I got off the train nobody was there. It was late and the dinky town was closed and dark. I hid my bag under the station and followed the road on the map he'd sent—on the map it said five miles but it must have been fifteen. Everywhere it was flat and as empty looking as out to sea. I could see the town there all the time and after so far it never seemed farther, like a wagon of lights that followed me all the way. There was a town off to the south but I never seemed to get closer—except for the telephone poles there was nothing around to go by. And then I would have walked past if the road hadn't ended there. He was just getting up and crossing the yard with a light. When he saw me he began to raise hell even before he was sure who I was, saying that now he'd have to go back in town for my bag. I didn't say anything so he held up the light and made sure. Then he said, *make yourself at home,* and walked away. There was no fire in the shack, which I thought was the garage, until I saw there was nothing else around. Just a privy and a shed off across the yard. He kept running up and down with a milk can like he was gassing a racing car and just left me standing there. Half the time I couldn't see him—just hear his heels on the ground. I'd been warm enough walking but standing there I began to freeze, and I went inside and warmed my hands on the lamp. There were two army cots, one on each side of the stove. A bear skin or something was spread on one but not even a blanket on the other—just an extra mattress with a big hole in the end. I sat down on it and four or five cats crawled out and meowed. Out in the yard an engine coughed, then after a bit went on coughing—sounding like something in a milk house, not on wheels. Then the lights came on and I could see his legs across the yard. He came and stopped in the door and looked at me. He was wearing a hunting cap with the red lining turned out and the ear muffs tied under his chin. Everything else was under stiff brown coveralls. He'd just got up yet his face was still covered with dust. "You want to take a try now," he said, "or you want to loaf awhile?" "I think maybe I'll just loaf awhile," I said. There was a caking of the dust around his teeth. Then he walked off without saying anything. He walked like a man who had a full can of milk in each hand and was afraid he'd spill a little if he didn't run.

"Bet he thinkin or dreamin," said Kirby, "—how he sure as hell seen life. Dreamin when he's out everybody be out—when he's free we all free. Same kind of thinkin I did when I was a kid. Thinkin that what I'd been through was through—through for everyone. And when I was a man then there couldn't be kids any more. He get free tomorrow an tear ass home thinkin tomorrow the Fourth of July, thinkin the whole goddam world just got out of jail an is free. But no fault of him feelin that way—he just doan know. You gotta come back two, three, four times before you know. You gotta forget half the things you learn before you know."

Sometimes I think if he'd thought of it first he'd been the world's greatest Christian—but since he didn't he had to think of something else. When it came to religion it had to be his or he wouldn't play. The rocks were a little miracle story all his own. He knew all the loose buttons on others and could snip them off with his thumb—without ever seeing his own pants were open all the time. He was the first man to try growing wheat instead of cattle right where everybody knew it couldn't be done. All by himself and a little woman called Vee. She ran the tractor days and he ran it nights. They lived in a tent and he just rented the land. The second year he made forty thousand dollars and sold the tent for thirty more right there in town. Then they were gone for three years till she died somewhere on an island—it was near Australia but not yet on the map, he said. When he came back the wheat idea was old stuff. He had to take a piece of land where it didn't rain. That was the winter I was there and left in the spring. I read two hundred of his little *Blue Books* and he read two to my one. We did nothing but read and plow and argue when it froze. The tractor never stopped for a week at a time and when I got off he got on, just around and around the fourteen hundred acres we had. The land had never been turned before and even the rabbits were surprised, scared at first, then moving just enough to let the plows by. And when I ate lunch they'd come and sit off where I could see the shine on their eyes—but when I popped at them with the gun the dust would spit halfway. No part of seeing was even the same out there. I saw things that weren't seeable before. I saw lakes floating on the land and cattle wading and the shadows of trees, and sometimes the house was lying in a pond of silver and gold. And sometimes the wind blew sound from my ears and the roar itself seemed quiet again and the yard was empty as clear water—till I moved from the door. Then a great flat hand pushed me on my face. Or across the yard to hang on the fence until I got down on my knees and crawled—and yet from the inside, through the window, nothing was there. Nothing—until I saw the cat belly squirming across the yard. That was where I really saw what reason was. No matter what a thing did, if it did it, a reason was there. Maybe I couldn't see it—but the thing was the reason itself. So now nothing was without a reason for me any more. If a thing was it had a reason, though it didn't follow that I'd find it out. It only followed that there was a reason there to find. And for both me and Uncle Dudley that was enough. Except for his rocks—which were for him like he was for me.

If there had been a rain we'd have split the $20,000 —but it didn't rain. I went back to Chicago and worked for Monkey Ward. I had a job in mail order shoes and ran around all day on skates, picking out shoes for little boys in Iowa. I lost about twenty-five of my hundred-thirty pounds in six weeks. And that was when instead of losing I should have put it on. One day I was standing in front of the Y eating a cake of Fleischmann's Yeast when Uncle Dudley drove up in a new Buick sedan. He was wearing a new pair of knickers and some sporty new shoes. His good-looking legs were even better looking than before. He stood a moment sizing me up, then he came over and pinched my seat. "You're lookin skinny as hell," he said and grinned at me. I felt so bad I couldn't even kid him back. He took my arm and we walked across the street to Joe's. We sat in a booth with a light on the table and had two steaks. Back then he was smoking Coronas and he lit one up. "I've got an idea, Kid—" he said, "how would you like to drive a car?" So in the morning six of us left for Florida.

"He likely dreamin," Kirby went on, "that this town really screwball—this town u-neek." He came over and looked down at me, then he walked to the door. He had good legs, fuzzy with crinkly hair, and he rubbed his hand up and down stirring it. When he stopped it went on wriggling like something alive. He had a shirt so thin the moonlight came through and his back was curved with the wrong muscles, all of them bending him over and none of them straightening him up. He kept one of the shirt tails out to wipe off his hands. "He likely dreamin—" he went on, "there nothin like this in the goddam world, and when he dream that he next dream that there nothin like us. An bygod, Hal—when he dreamin that he close to true. Maybe we ain't bad but there ain't much good in us. The thing about us is we no goddam use to our kind. There birds that eat bugs off the trees but there no birds for us. We here because we really no good—no good to our kind. Even Furman out spittin in eyes is no good to our kind—"

"Furman only man I know who really more somethin than what he ain't."

"I know—I know, Furman all right—Furman a really brave man. But what Furman is somethin more is thirty days more every month. What the hell good it do all his goddam spittin in eyes? Me an you not so brave, not out spittin, but we all sittin here—"

"The truth—" said Hal. "But Furman still somethin more than what he ain't—"

"When we out—" said Kirby, "we drunk—an when we drunk we back in here. But in or out we no dam good to our kind. We say—so long, boys, see you in hell—an then bygod that's where we do— for where else I ever see you, Hal, 'cept back up here? We think we all goin our ways but we doan see our ways are goin the same. We all just goin nowhere an we all too dam dumb to see. But everybody else see it—an this kid likely dreamin it now. It plain we no good—what difference it make thinkin about how? We no good to our kind, any kind, an since we no good we here. Maybe I only met one or two some good people in all my life. Maybe Furman is one, maybe sometime he nearly two. Then I ask myself— Furman, what good all this spittin doin our kind? An what Furman say?—he spit. He lean an spit in some eye."

"Kirby, you ain't so dumb."

182

"I here, ain't I?"

"So Furman here."

"Furman's a reason."

"You a reason too—we all admirin your tellin 'em off."

"I tell 'em off?"

"You was good as hell. We all sayin we never heard such good tellin off."

"Too bad I so drunk I didn't hear."

"That what Furman say. Furman say what use tellin 'em off when you really doan know."

"Furman like it?"

"He 'bout to died."

"Then there some use tellin 'em off. But Furman right—"

"That what Dewey say. Dewey say Furman there an tell 'em off at same time."

"How that funny old man that laugh—one in the little boy's pants?"

"He quiet now—he quiet as hell. He like Peanut some the way he laugh—but I declare he old enough to know."

"Where he lyin now?"

"He next to Furman—he lyin with his feet up like somethin dead."

Kirby left the door and walked to look at him. Uncle Dudley made a noise and rolled on his face. He made so much noise I knew he wasn't asleep but lying there thinking about him an old man in little boy's pants. He'd been called worse than that but it's different when you're not called that—but just hear it. There's something worse than being called something about that. Like me hearing that I'm such a kid, as if I didn't know it—and yet I didn't want to know it just that way.

"He likely dreamin just what the kid dreamin—that an what a fine story he got to tell. Take out the map an show everybody just where it was. Tell 'em all how brave an funny as hell he was. How him an a little kid died laughin an everybody else just sick an glum. Tell 'em how it's all in the game—kinda game he learned to play. An he go on thinkin his brave little game is enough. Thing is, we know we no good, Hal—but little shorty pants here still think he hot stuff. Never know he no good at all for any dam kind."

Uncle Dudley rolled over and his toes pointed up. I looked hard but all I could see was Kirby's striped shorts and Uncle Dudley's socks—I raised my head so I wouldn't miss what Uncle Dudley would say. But a funny thing, he didn't say a word. He didn't breathe heavy or make any noise, he just lay there. I kept listening till my neck was sore, then I lay back and closed my eyes. I heard Kirby's feet go across the floor, heard him get in bed. I tried to think where I'd left off thinking of my Uncle Dudley. But when he hadn't said anything he'd shut that off too. I heard Peanut roll over and knew he was watching but I couldn't move to look at him. Then I thought—since I'm Uncle Dudley so much, maybe he's some of me. Maybe that was the part of him that was silent now. Maybe there was something of what we both were in not being brave—we wanted to be brave but we wanted out even more. And like he told me once, what we want to be most is what we are. And now maybe I think a really brave man doesn't want to be brave. He just wants to be something else first and brave tags along. He just wants to be *something*— and we don't know what it is. Sometime I think we'd both like to see what that kind of want is. For that kind of want would be my Uncle Dudley and me on a horse.

I woke up hearing him walking up and down the floor. His shoes were on but he hadn't laced them and the heels dragged on the floor, the laces noisy and flapping on the toes. He hadn't buckled his knickers either and the straps were loose and slapping —he hummed *Annie Laurie* but away off tune. When *Annie Laurie* came in he said it like he really meant it, but the rest of time just hummed it through his nose. One at a time I heard them all roll over and look. The moon was low now and bright on him when he turned in the door, green on his head and his thin hair like bubbles in ice. I could hear Hal wet his lips and Dewey softly swear. I waited for Peanut, but he just lay wide-eyed and stared. Dragging his heels and humming Uncle Dudley walked up and down. Then Red suddenly sat up like someone had kicked him in his sleep and Uncle Dudley stopped at the door, took a long look outside. I knew he looked funny but he'd never looked old before. Moonlight wasn't his kind of light any more. But he closed his eyes and took a deep breath like that air was fresher—then raising his arms did his bending exercise. Right at the floor he cheated like he always did. He did ten which was five too many and then leaning back he looked all around—he was breathing heavy and his vest front went up and down. He tried to stand straight and look broad shouldered but one knee gave away. He held on to the bars and I could see his heart pound in his wrist.

"We seen it," said Red. "We seen all ten—now suppose you lace them goddam shoes." My Uncle Dudley waited a moment, then he turned around.

"Now my boy," he said, but it sounded quakey and he coughed. "My boy—" he went on, "don't let it get you down. Or if you must don't blame it on me," he said, "—or us." He put out his arm and moved it to take all of us in. But it went out of the light and he had to draw it in to see—there was a bite on the back of one finger and he scratched at it.

"Bygod—" said Red. "You must be drunk. You know goddam well who ain't takin it now. You know all this hummin and flappin ain't takin, but givin it out." Uncle Dudley just stood looking at his hand.

He turned to the door like the light there was better —he scratched it once, then he lifted it to his mouth.

"Leave the old man alone," said Dewey. "Only wish bygod that I was as drunk. Take a dam good man to be drunk an walkin like that. Take a dam good man to hold it an walk it up—"

"That old fool ain't drunk," said Red, "—but bygod for once bet he wishes he was. How about it—?" said Red, looking up, "how about a little nip now?" Uncle Dudley turned around with his back to the light. He took his finger out of his mouth and held it out where the wetness showed, then he raised it like the words were on the way. But before he got one of them out somebody coughed. It was a real cough— yet you knew something else was on hand. I'd never heard it before but I knew that on first hearing, and Uncle Dudley knew it and we turned our heads. We looked back where the only light was the stool and paper on the floor.

"I regret it," said the voice, "—an I feel for you. When a man's feelins are hard to bear he takes a nip— a nip or two. An sometimes they hard to bear they so good, sometimes they so bad. But havin hard-to-bear feelins ain't what makes a man a dam fool. It's havin people who hold such feelins agen the law." The man was in the booth with the door closed, beside the stool. He talked slow like he made the words first in the back of his mouth.

"Furman," said Hal. "This ain't that kind of

187

drunk. This the kind of drunk just from feelins alone. This the kind of feelin but without any drinkin at hand."

"All the same," said Furman, "he drunk. He drunk like someone say."

Uncle Dudley turned to look at his hand again. He spread the fingers and held it right up close to his face.

"You drunk too?" said Red.

"I often been—"

"We all been," said Hal. "But Furman not in for drinkin—Furman in for spittin in eyes."

"Who?" said Red.

"He spit 'em all—"

"Ain't yet spit Cupid," Furman said.

"Cupid ain't come close," said Dewey. "Let him come close an Furman spit in his eye."

"That I will," Furman said.

"That's dam pretty soundin all right," said Red, "but what in the hell good it do you—what you doin it for?"

"They been pickin on him," said Dewey. "They keep pickin on him cause Furman won't mind. They say Furman—you get the hell outa town an you stay out till we lettin you in. They say Furman gotta learn his place—an Furman say his place here. He say his place come to be wherever such basterds is."

"That it is," said Furman.

"Very nice," said Red, "but just what the hell good

188

does it do?" Uncle Dudley was looking at the moon. He blinked his eyes and nodded like he saw an old friend there. He put his hands down and bent some at the knees.

"What we been tellin him three months now," Dewey said. "But he no sooner out than he back in. Once he out he right off spittin in eyes. Last time it was McCord—"

"Since then McCord been sick lookin—"

"He dyin," said Furman, "he dyin from the inside out. He so sick sometimes he smell already dead—"

"That he do, that he really do," said Hal.

"But Biscuit half all right," said Dewey. "Biscuit some like his old man."

"When a man paid for being sick," said Furman, "he gonna be sick a long time. All my life I been paid for a horse an I been a good horse up to now. Up to now I never seen what a dam good horse I was."

"Ain't it the truth," said Hal. Uncle Dudley turned from the moon and looked inside. He started to move but his shoes were noisy and he stopped, turned back again. I thought I heard Peanut but when I looked his eyes were closed.

"I know'd you, Hal, since you pee'd on my sleeve when your Ma come payin a call—an bygod if you ain't most what you are cause you never been paid. I bet you feelin you good as lost in this world. Bein paid for a horse I knew my place but you lost cause

189

you never been paid. Bet you half the time just lyin aroun thinkin that you no dam good."

"Furman, you close to true—"

"Same with Dewey some. 'Cept he bein paid for bein an ass an he been a good ass up to now."

"Only half the time I ain't been paid."

"Trouble is you so goddam easy-goin nothin really get to eatin you. You as soon live in here as outside. Likely when you out you really feelin more lost than when you at home up here. No Biscuit out there to daddy you. You have to go an find a bed of your own. You act really mad an shoot off some but it all like flushin the water crapper here. You really somethin like Biscuit at heart. You really nice boy but if your belly full you put up with all the pushin aroun. You doan mean no harm but you no dam good." Dewey stopped rolling his cigarette. He held the paper curled on his finger, the pouch string in his teeth. "How many time I lie here hearin you—hearin all of you that come in. You gonna be tough—an when you out you gonna raise hell. Lyin here seems like I never heard so many brave men. Yet you been in and out same as me. But I ain't yet heard of all your hell to pay. Guess it just doan eat at you like it does me. I ain't brave—I scared wet all the time—but I really scared most of bein out free. Of bein outside for what I didn't do instead of here for what I did. McCord really sick—but he look right well beside that part of

190

me. An anybody who stand aroun takin his sass is sicker than McCord."

"Rooster!" said Uncle Dudley, and pointed like he could see. He kept his hand out pointing and turned to look around. "Rooster—" he said, "soon be—" Peanut rolled on his face. He made no sound but his feet kicked in the light, fast like he was learning how to swim. The White Owl band came off and rolled out on the floor. When he stopped kicking we could hear the thin Peanut sound.

"That boy got somethin," said Furman. "I wouldn't know—but he got somethin there. It really funny, funny like he say. How you like it here, boy?" he said.

"I 'bout to die laughin," Peanut said.

"But this kinda joke tire you after while. But I declare I plumb forgot it was a joke."

"Gettin back—" said Dewey, "gettin back to tellin off—suppose you do some tellin off about you. You still a horse or you now changin some?"

"There a horse I once seen that was up front a man. Wun't a real horse, just a picture horse I seen. But that the kinda horse I now think I am."

"Kirby wanta be that kinda horse too."

"Kirby all right," said Dewey. "Kirby been aroun—"

"He been in Texas—he been in Rome."

"He say the purtiest thing he ever seen some island off there. Sittin off in water so blue it'd stain your hand. An a mountain sittin there an smokin all the time."

"Like a feather, he say—smokin like a feather."

"Purtiest thing I seen a young bull at the Fair."

"Some bulls is purty."

"—just everything where it belonged."

"Like a woman I seen walkin in Mobile. Never seen so much woman in all my life. An there she was walkin a know-nothin man. A love-turned woman an a know-nothin man—"

"Purtiest thing," said Furman, "—bunch of leghorns I seen."

"Furman," said Hal. "We way head of leghorns now. We talkin 'bout 'nother chicken now."

"—just before dark," Furman went on. "An I declare I never seen white before. Them chickens was like holes in the ground. They make ordinary white like in here. And there they were, all messin aroun. Purtiest thing I seen." Uncle Dudley turned from the door again. His mouth was open and he was raising his hand . . .

"I a dog," said Peanut. "Purtiest thing I ever seen. He smooth as a grass bank in the rear. He born 'thout a tail an smooth in the rear. Everyone say he a new kinda dog. Purtiest thing anywhere I seen."

"You young," said Dewey. "You change from dogs in time. There no kind of purty like the woman I seen. So every which way purty I just had to stand back—"

192

"Real purty," said Furman, "kind that make you stand back. Ain't purty just to make a man hot at all. No more than a bitch purty in the heat. Every kinda dog just taggin aroun."

"Ain't purty—" said Hal, "but funniest thing I seen—"

"What that?" said Dewey.

"How we all talkin here. Lyin here in the dark an all this long talkin here—"

"What funny 'bout that?"

"I doan know—seem funny to me. Day time all we say goddam—night time we lie talkin here."

"I ain't noticed we special quiet in the day."

"But night talkin," said Hal, "—seem to be sayin more'n it's sayin."

Uncle Dudley sat down. He sat down on Peanut's bed and bent over to lace his shoes. He tied the bows very careful and tucked in the loose ends. He stretched out one leg to buckle his knicker at the knee.

"But 'fore we through now, Furman," said Dewey, "there one thing I wanta be tellin you. You really all right, Furman, but there some things you just doan know. You say that you in and out but the thing about you—you out while you in. All you talkin suit you fine but how the hell it suit Hal and me? Hal and me here all the time we here. We ain't brave as you—but still we here. An we ain't really bad—but still we here. We easy-goin as hell but we still got feelins an when you feelin like me you ain't spittin in eyes. Spittin in eyes is really spittin in your own. I really glad I'm easy-goin as you say. If I wasn't easy-goin bygod I'd go nuts. We all trapped, Furman, an spittin won't make us free. Somebody got to play the sucker an if it ain't you it's me. An if it ain't me or Hal—then there two more just like us here. An what good all the spittin doin you or doin me? An if it ain't me an you—what good the spittin doin them?"

Uncle Dudley stood up and smoothed his knickers at the knee. Then he walked very slow, his hand out, toward the white stool. One shoe squeaked but nothing flapped anywhere. At the stool he stopped and began to take off his coat. His vest was dark but I could see his white sleeves.

"Hearin you now—" said Furman, "make me see how little time I had. For all the thinkin I need two months in here ain't enough. There more than one thing true an I sure that true for you—but you wrong to think my true ain't for spittin in eyes. For spittin in eyes is just what I been called on to do, an what a man really called on for he must. An I come to see I called on to do it now. Since I'm a new kinda horse I need a new kinda feed."

"Make me sick," said Dewey, "—see you out again spittin in eyes."

"There just Cupid," said Furman, "—then I done what I called on to do."

194

Dewey rolled over and spit against the wall. I could see Uncle Dudley's arms go up and hear his coat hang on a nail. He made a noise like yawning but it wasn't a yawn and like coughing but it wasn't a cough. I heard the buckle flap loose in his belt. A rooster crowed and right below one answered, the hens making a shuffling sound. Then a light went on somewhere. I felt Red turn and put his hat on his face and then half roll over toward me. The light came in the window and the door. It reached way in and yellow'd the stool and Uncle Dudley's pale, plump knees, bright on his stringy lick of hair. His face was in his hands, the fingers tight over his eyes, too quiet for a man just sitting there. Maybe he felt me looking, I don't know. Maybe it was just the light, warm on his knees. But there was a door on a wire and without looking he fumbled at it, let it slowly swing closed. Underneath his pants settled on the floor. Then I heard Peanut turn from looking at him and roll on his side to look at me. I closed my eyes and began to breathe out loud.

2

WHEN I WOKE UP Red moved over for me to scratch him, but when I did he itched all over right away. It was morning now and the light was back on. The glare was gone, not even shadows any more—I could look right at it and see the wires inside. Dewey was just sitting there on his bed. When I coughed he looked at me but he didn't see anything and then he spit on the floor and looked at that. He didn't look the same in the morning light. He turned the front of his underwear back and there they were, crawling, he just took the big one—let him go along his thumb to the right place then mashed him. He opened the other side up and I looked at Hal. Hal was lying on his back and his mouth and eyes were a little open, but just open, not looking at anything. He didn't look the same either somehow. Peanut was lying asleep on his face. Uncle Dudley was sprawled asleep on the floor. He lay on the mattress in the corner with the stool, like he'd got soft and melted there, one arm stiff and twisted around. One hand stuck out like a man sneaking up behind. His hat was in the

196

puddle that leaked out from the rear, tipped so I could see his initials and the toothpicks in the band.

"Mornin," she said, and when I turned, put a basket down. She must have just been standing there for I hadn't heard her come up at all and she was black as the bars against the light. Her dress was clean and sticking out front from the fresh ironing, her dark green bloomers showing underneath. Dewey got up and walked over and looked at her. She looked up at him through glasses with bright silver rims—but if there were any lenses they didn't show. Just the bottom-side whites of her big eyes. "An how Dewey?" she said. But Dewey didn't say. He leaned on the bars and looked over her head at the wall. He had on his pants and shoes and he didn't scratch, just stood leaning there. 'How many you now?" she said, and moved to one side so she could see. She lifted her glasses and squinted in at us. " 'Nother li'l boy," she said. "Where they findin so many li'l boys?" She looked up at Dewey then back again at me. "You like egg, li'l boy?"

I didn't say anything.

"He likes *eggs* better," said Red. "How about you bringin us little boys half dozen fried eggs?" She looked at Red, then back at Dewey again.

"That a sailah boy?" she said.

"We're both little sailor boys," said Red, "but we ain't so little we ain't hungry as hell."

She took tin cups from the basket and set them on

197

the floor. She took the lid from a tin pail and filled all the cups about even, then she took one and filled it to the brim. "That for Furman. How Furman? Furman eatin his egg?" Dewey didn't answer so she looked up at him. He nodded his head and she pushed the cups under the door. She had long braids and when she stooped they spilled out in front, waving little white ribbons at each end. "So Furman eatin his egg," she said. "Now I declare—he comin along. You think Furman eat some chittlin cookin now?" Dewey was picking up two cups and nodded again. She went away with her basket and Dewey gave one cup to Hal, drank the other one right down himself. Hal just leaned on his elbow, smelling it. Dewey took the full one to Furman and just pushed it under the door, waiting till Furman picked it up, then walking away. He took off his shoes and lay back in bed, turning from the light.

Red got up and got one for himself and me. He went and looked at Uncle Dudley, then came back and shook his head. It tasted like some stuff I had in Hannibal one time. It was coffee all right but the beans were green instead of roasted—and though I couldn't take it then I took it now. It tasted like soap I once ate and won a pitcher's glove.

Chickens were noisy somewhere and windows went up and down. A woman came out and made clucking sounds and raising on one arm I could see her—she was feeding leghorns and they looked like Furman

198

had said. Whiter than white against the dark ground —but with dirty behinds. When I turned back the colored girl was there with her basket again. She just stood there looking in, like people look at a litter of something, something they'd been waiting for and just now had. But she looked at Red more than she looked at me. She was maybe no older than me but there was no way to tell it—when she said little boy she meant that was how I looked to her. She didn't mean she wanted to show she was older and such.

"You got us sailor boys eggs?" said Red, trying to sound like Hal and Dewey.

"You get a egg—that all anyone get."

"Well—dish it up," said Red, "before it cackles an grows feathers."

She didn't think it was funny—she didn't think it was anything. She put the basket down and took out one tin plate. "Where Dewey?" she said. Dewey rolled over and put on his shoes. He walked to the door and she slipped it under to him. "That for Furman," she said. "That what he get for eatin his egg." Dewey picked it up and walked back to Furman's booth.

"Furman," he said, "here you egg. Here you egg an somethin special for you. Abby cooked you some chittlin that make you belly turn."

"Abby," Furman said, "I declare you spoilin me."

" 'Tain't nothin," Abby said.

"I heard it often said some black folks nighin on to white. But I ain't yet heard what I'm goin to say.

That bein there dam few white folks nighin on to black."

"Abby so black," said Dewey, "even black folks nighin on." Abby laughed. She put her hand up like to hide behind it and turned away. "She whiter than leghorns—" Furman said, "them leghorns I seen."

Abby covered her ears and closed her eyes very tight. Then she remembered her mouth was open and closed that too. Then she let her ears peek and not hearing anything she opened her eyes, took out all of the plates and slid them under the door. There was an egg and some grits and two slices of white bread. Without moving from bed Peanut reached one across the floor, propping it up even with his mouth. There was a fork but he just left it there. He mixed the mush and the egg and scraped it into his mouth with the crust. He saved the center till the last and nibbled at it. Hal lay on his stomach and left the pan on the floor. He ate very slow and sometimes lay back and closed his eyes. Dewey had to go to the stool and sat and ate his there. Red ate my grits and I ate one of his pieces of bread.

When Peanut finished nibbling the center he put the piece of crust inside of a paper bag he had in his shirt. He took out a dry piece and lay back and sucked on it. He didn't look like a kid to die laughing any more. His hair was stiff and brittle like straw, and he peeked out from under it like from a hole. There was a sore on his ear and he kept picking at it.

Kirby sat up like in his sleep and sucked the yellow right out of the egg, then he threw the pan and the mush against the wall. There were caked spots all around like he'd done it before. He looked at the new spot awhile then he lay back. Nobody said anything but when Dewey finished he picked up the pan, made a pile of them near the door. There was one left but he let it set there. There was a coffee too, but he drank that and pushed the cup through the door. Then he walked back and lay down on his bed.

It got so quiet I could hear Red breathe. It was noisy outside but didn't seem to get inside at all— Peanut stopped sucking his bread and I could hear the stool. Only Uncle Dudley was like being alive any more. He made a noise like a leak, then another noise like cleaning it up; that and the sound of the stool was all there was. Then Dewey got up and walked over to look at him. He looked at him awhile then he stooped over and picked up his hat. Holding it like a newspaper he tore it in half. Then he tore those parts in half and all of it in half once more. He picked them all up and took them and dumped them in the stool. He let the water run and it flushed three times before it ran over, spreading a pool around Uncle Dudley's feet. Then he turned it off and came out and looked at him. His knickers were soft woolly stuff and soaked some of it up like a blotter, turning dark clear around in front and up his knee. Without looking at anyone Dewey got back in bed. Once I thought I heard Peanut laugh but I couldn't move to look at him and Red was lying back with his eyes tight closed. I went on looking at Uncle Dudley and after while he began to snore.

A car came into the yard and honked its horn. Someone opened a door and the car backed out and drove away. Two men just stood and talked at the foot of the stairs. One kept saying *uhuh* like a man who isn't listening and the other one talked like he knew that was how it was. He was saying that upstairs now there just wasn't room. He kept saying there just wasn't room—there just wasn't room. No room? said the other one. No—no room, he said. Then bygod we'll make room, said the other one—won't we now? He said yes and then he walked away.

Dewey got up very fast and put on his shoes. Hal sat up and looked at him. He cleared his throat like he meant to talk and looked around like the room was changed, like the sun had come in somewhere. But Dewey didn't look at him. He walked across and stood in the door, buttoning his pants. He made a noise like he'd just been asleep then he yawned very loud and said *BOY*. Then he said— "Well if it ain't my old pal Chief McBee."

"How my boy Dewey?" said McBee.

"Fine as hell," said Dewey. "I really fine as hell."

"How resta my boys?"

"We all fine—"

202

"I treat you good—doan I now?"

"You square as hell—you O.K."

"How my boy Hal?"

"I fine—" said Hal, and sat up blinking his eyes. "An how you?" Chief McBee didn't say. Hal got out of bed and put on his pants, walked barefoot to the door.

"I seen you old man," said McBee. "He ask about you—I said you fine."

"I swell as hell."

"What I told him. I said I treat my boys fine— you ask 'em, I said—doan I now?"

"This like a home," Dewey said.

"The truth," said Hal.

"How my boy Kirby?"

"He sleepin yet—"

"Now Kirby doan treat me fair. He gotta learn, doan he now?"

"That he do—"

"Kirby gotta pay."

"The truth," said Hal.

The one with the keys came out again, shaking them on a ring. They both came up the stairs and stood on the landing—they peeked in, shading their eyes. Biscuit had the keys and he put one in the door. Chief McBee followed him in.

"How my new boys?" he said.

We didn't say anything. There was egg on his

mouth and he chewed on a match; he spit it out and took another one.

"How my new boys!" he said.

"They all right," said Hal.

"They nice boys," said Dewey.

"Get up!" said McBee. I got up, Red just sat there. He acted like he was fixing his shoes; he shined them a bit then stood up.

"Where you papers you—" said McBee, and stuck out his head at Red.

"You've got 'em," said Red. "If nobody down there can read 'em I'll read 'em to you." McBee just stared at him. Then he turned to Biscuit—

"He got papers?" he said.

"Yeah," said Biscuit. "He been discharged."

"That what they all say—they all say been discharged—we check up on him first. Doan we now—?"

"I'm checkin up," Biscuit said.

"This other boy nice."

"Sure," said Biscuit. They both stood and looked at me. McBee's eyes jumped around like the match jumped in his mouth. He spit it out and stepped on the head until it caught fire on the floor, then he stood back and watched it burn. When it went out he put a new one in his mouth.

"How many comin in?" he said.

"Three—" said Biscuit. "Anyhow three." McBee turned and looked around the room. He saw Uncle

Dudley asleep on the floor and went over to look at him. He stood on the edge of the pool and sniffed at him.

"Who this?" he said.

"He the old man," said Biscuit. "He the old man that go with the boy."

"Get up!" said McBee. My Uncle Dudley didn't move. He'd stopped snoring but made a little slobber noise. "Get him up!" yelled McBee, and looked at Biscuit, waving his arms. Biscuit walked over and stood looking down at him. Then he bent over and tapped Uncle Dudley on his wet knee. "Oh gee-*zus*-crist—" said McBee, and looked around for something to swing. There was a piece of broom in by the stool, the broom end worn and smooth as a paddle, and he ran in for it then ran right out again. But when he got out Uncle Dudley was just standing there. He was breathing a little hard but he looked like he'd always been there. Something had bit him under one eye and it was swelled shut and his face was dirty—some of the water ran down his leg and some dripped on the floor. He looked like hell if I'd ever seen him look that way. He looked as different now as they all did, the room, the whole works. And yet he looked something like Uncle Dudley just the same.

"O.K.," said McBee, dropping the broom, "get 'em outa here—take 'em outa town." Biscuit took my Uncle Dudley's arm and led him to the door. McBee stopped beside me and looked at Peanut's bed. He didn't look at Peanut—just blinked at Peanut's bare feet. Peanut sat up and covered them. "How you like it here, kid—how you like it?" said McBee.

"I 'bout to die laughin," Peanut said. He wasn't laughing at all and his eyes looked wet but he didn't blink them—he just sat and stared.

"If you gonna die," said McBee, turning away and looking at Dewey. "If you gonna die you might as well die here—"

"This a nice place to die," Dewey said. McBee looked at Hal and Hal turned away. "This like dyin at home," Dewey said.

"Who else here?" said McBee, and looked back at Biscuit. Biscuit pushed his hat back and looked at Red. When McBee looked at him Red sat down. "I tell you to sit?" said McBee, looking off again at Biscuit.

"I quit a good job," said Red, "so I could do my own standin and sittin. And bygod that's just what I'm doin now." McBee spit the new match out on the floor. He stepped on it like it was alive and might bite, but it only sputtered.

"That just fine," said McBee. "There plenty room for sittin an standin up here. There plenty room up here for my boys—ain't there now?"

"Sure—" Dewey said.

"An now who?" said McBee, and looked back toward the stool.

"There me," said Dewey.

206

"An Furman—" said Hal.

McBee was looking right at the door. "Bycrist—" he said. "My old pal Furman. Thinka me forgettin Furman—how you, Furman?"

"I sick to retchin," said Furman, "—from your sass."

"Bygod, Furman, now you listen—"

"I enough. I sick to retchin now."

"Furman, you payin now an bygod you gonna pay. You gonna pay an you gonna keep payin—Furman, you hear?"

"Hearin you talk make me full this kinda pay. I really got more this kinda pay than there place to spend—"

"Bygod, Furman," said McBee, but he couldn't go on. "Bygod—" he said.

"I gonna retch," said Furman. "I gonna get up an retch in you eye." McBee turned and bumped into Biscuit, squeezed through the door. He half stumbled on the stairs, then crossed the yard and got in the car—the door swung open and he got out again, went inside.

"Now how 'bout me?" said Dewey. "You just two now—how 'bout me?"

"Take him," said Furman. "Take him if he promise to leave town. McBee make me retch but Dewey make me sick at heart. He make me sick down where it won't retch up." Dewey walked out on the landing and down the stairs. He waited at the bottom for

Uncle Dudley, Biscuit and me. Uncle Dudley had to take his time and stumbled once on the bottom stair. His eye was watering some and made a streak on his face. Dewey got in the car, then Uncle Dudley, then me. Biscuit went around and got in up front. Cupid was sitting there like half asleep, his face very pink, some nice-smelling powder where his neck was sore. Red stood at the window and looked at me. He didn't look mad or anything, just looked like he was trying to think. Hal was standing behind him, smiling some. Like in his dream seeing people come home, now he was seeing them go away, glad for them, but sorry to see them go. Biscuit started the car and we backed out of the yard.

We stopped on the street next to the levee and Dewey got out.

"I like you, Dewey," Biscuit said, "but you really wearin Furman down. You hard on Furman an now you be right back."

"No—" said Dewey. "I leavin—honest to God I leavin right now." Biscuit gave him two cigarettes and Dewey walked away. When I looked back he was on the corner, lighting one. Uncle Dudley took out his cigar and it was half smoked and crushed—he started to light it up then he threw the match away. He took a bite off the soggy end and began to chew. We went along with one wheel in the grass and Cupid got sleepy again. He leaned his gun over against Biscuit and crossed his arms on his chest. Uncle Dudley's mouth was full and he spit, wiped it with his hand.

"Well, Kid—" he said, "we'd better spit up."

"Spit up—?" I said.

"Split up," he said. "Out here we bitter split up. Nobody'll risk pickin two of us up and we'll get along faster that way."

"Sure," I said.

"You'll be at the Y?"

"I'll be at the Y in three days," I said. Uncle Dudley put his hand on my head.

"Any plugs to spare, Kid?" he said.

"Not now," I said. He laughed and mussed up my hair. Then he stuck in his fingers where it was thick and pulled out some. He made a little brown ring of it and put it away in his vest.

"O.K.," said Biscuit, pulling off the road. "An now don't you boys waste any time. We be drivin by here in an hour or so an—"

"Nice place to drive," Uncle Dudley said. That was the first time he'd sounded like Uncle Dudley and I looked at him, but he was backing out the door. I got out and stood in the ditch grass and he leaned on the running board. He just stayed there looking at Cupid and once Cupid looked at him.

"O.K.—now beat it!" Cupid said. He turned and grinned at Biscuit and Biscuit began to laugh. They both laughed but Uncle Dudley laughed even more. When they stopped he kept right on laughing like it was the best thing he'd ever heard. Cupid leaned on the door and looked at him. The cigar juice was leaking on Uncle Dudley's chin and he looked like hell yet he looked kind of sporty. He tipped his head and winked at Cupid with his good eye. Cupid thought that was pretty funny and winked back at him—then he closed one eye and opened the other one wide. And right when he did Uncle Dudley spit him, full flush in that eye. The juice spattered all over his face and dripped dark brown on his front—but he didn't move, he just sat stiff, his hands white on the door. Then suddenly he reached for the gun, but Biscuit had it, pointing it at the sky. He made motions with it for Uncle Dudley to get in. "Easy now—easy, easy, easy now," he said. "Easy, boy—"

Uncle Dudley turned and spit the rest in the road, hitched up his pants. He didn't look at me but climbed inside and closed the door. He sat back behind the side curtain so I couldn't see. Biscuit put the gun on the floor and Cupid kept his head down, just his red neck showing. Biscuit backed the car around and they slowly moved away. In the rear view mirror I could see him looking back at me. They went along with a wheel in the road grass like we had come. The wind was faster now and went by, stirring a kind of dust on the road, getting thick, then petering out where the pavement began. On the turn my Uncle Dudley put out his hand.